Reva's River

Virginia Babcock

Cover Art:
Michelle Crocker

http://mlcdesigns4you.weebly.com/

Publisher's Note:

This is a work of fiction. All names, characters, places, and
events are the work of the author's imagination.

Any resemblance to real persons, places, or events is
coincidental.

Solstice Publishing - www.solsticepublishing.com

Reva's River
Virginia Babcock

Reva's River

Chapter One
Robert, Alan and Sparky

"Alan, hold on, man." Robert Leland spoke quietly into the tiny radio transmitter near his jaw. He lay on the floor at the rear of Renata's Grocery and Butcher's in a DC suburb. He, and his partner Alan were working undercover as part of an FBI investigation into the Renata brothers' crime ring. For six long months, both agents had been working their way into the Renata family's army of low-level enforcers. Then something had happened last night, at a poker game.

At a local bar owned by the Renatas, a group of about a dozen toughs had met for their weekly Saturday night poker game. Saturdays were a busy day for the Renata brothers, and they preferred that the spare toughs be available in case something went down. The brothers used poker both to entertain their crews as well as to keep them busy and out of trouble on quiet Saturday nights.

Alan and Robert had split and each was a member of two different five-man teams. Each boss would take a bodyguard, a driver, and maybe a second, and one 'team' when leaving Renata territory. Robert and Alan had worked hard and succeeded in infiltrating different teams or crews, so that they could each accompany one of the many Renata brothers when they went out to a meeting or event.

Robert's crew had arrived late to the poker game. His crew wasn't the last though; Alan's crew hadn't yet arrived. Robert mingled at the fringes with the other toughs and sipped a whisky sour while watching the barmaid make her way through the tables on her way to get more drinks. Everyone was enjoying the excitement of Saturday night. Something always happened on Saturday night. Either the bosses had some enemies for them to take out, or a big meeting was going down. If not, someone could always win a nice cut on one of the poker hands. No poker yet, because Alan's crew was in charge of the chips tonight. Alan's lieutenant, Sparky, ranked higher than the others, and was subsequently tasked to hold the chips and the 'house's' bankroll. The Renata brothers subsidized the games as a way to pass bonuses on to the crews.

Robert heard a few comments about the late crew, but no one was upset yet. The drinks had just started, and though no one was stupid enough to get drunk, enough alcohol had flowed to loosen up the guys.

An hour later, Sparky and the crew finally arrived. Sparky was flushed and had a bright look in his eye, as he passed a bundled roll of cash to all of the crews' members, "Sorry ladies, Boss wanted to give everyone something special tonight to celebrate the big deal he closed with the Connolly clan this fine day." Robert and Alan cheered with the rest and accepted a roll each. Robert surreptitiously flicked through his roll of bills before tucking it into his inner jacket pocket. He'd have to count it later, but the roll was one and a half inches thick, and seemed to be all twenties. "Quite a haul," Robert thought. He caught Alan's eye and nodded. They would need to meet later tonight. They knew as all the other toughs did, the Renatas always gave out wads of money before a big action. In this way, the toughs would have a last night out or their family members would have a small nest egg if their fellow didn't return home the next day. The larger-than-normal size of this roll meant that this would be a quiet Saturday night, because something big was going down on Sunday or Monday.

Once Sparky had wet his throat with a beer, he signaled his second to load the tables, and the poker night began. Everyone relaxed into a game knowing no action would happen tonight. Everyone knew their captain would instruct them in the morning of their part in whatever was going down. Veterans played hard, or stayed back, based on their personality. The size of the bankroll told the veterans that at least half of them wouldn't survive the next day.

Later that night, after the games ended and the bar emptied, Robert waited in his beat down apartment a few blocks down from the bar. Alan knocked on the door with his typical signal. Robert opened it quickly and pulled Alan in. Quietly they checked the room for bugs and the windows for watchers as they sat at the rickety kitchen table in plain sight of the front window and pantomimed a couple of guys talking over a beer.

Robert opened their conversation as he sipped his non-alcoholic beer, "Sparky give you any clues?"

"Not really. The two eldest brothers were both in the office when they called him in. I saw a couple of the other lieutenants, but they closed the door quickly. One of the other guys got excited. He told me that the bosses typically called all the lieutenants into a close-door meeting when planning a strategy for an upcoming altercation with another syndicate. When Sparky came out, we headed to the bar, but the other guys were real quiet, so I followed suit. Some of the nervous ones got the courage up to talk, and one speculated that now that the Connollys were falling in line that maybe the Renatas would take over their turf despite the deal. Sparky turned back and looked him in the eye, and smiling mean when he said 'Garcia, you know better. We'll keep the deal, but if the Connollys want to rumble tomorrow, we'll rumble."

"So, do you think they'll renege tomorrow and take them down?"

Alan shook his head. "I don't know. But, I got a bad feeling. Sparky had us take the van today *and* he stopped at the grocery after meeting the bosses. We stayed in the van while Sparky had the driver stop out back, and then he jumped out telling the driver to give him two minutes. Sparky came back with three of the Renatas' personal crew. I recognized one as being way high in the organization.

Then, the four of them took eight big duffel bags from the back of our van into the storage room. Those bags were big, and could have held guns. We were in one of the big 15-passenger crew vans,"

Robert interrupted his partner, "One where the Renatas removed the back two benches?"

"It was."

The crash of someone kicking in the apartment door cut off Alan's explanation. Robert and Alan only had time to stand up from the table and grab for their guns when Sparky and three unfamiliar toughs broke into the apartment. The agents stood at opposite sides of the table as they tried to fend off the attackers, but one used a set of brass knuckles on Robert's temple while another whacked Alan across his guts with a baseball bat and then brought it down on his head when he bent over clutching his middle.

Chapter Two
Who Made It Out

Robert lay in the uncomfortably noisy hospital bed. He hated its clammy feel against his skin and the constant noise from the circulating air within the mattress. The constant movement was supposed to keep him from getting bedsores and blood clots, but it was a damned nuisance. The plastic covered by a sheet didn't breathe and made him sweaty despite the bedding and padding. Then at night, when they'd put the calf cuff on his good leg, it would inflate and deflate all night long and jar him out of sleep. What little he got, that was. *Not that the nightmares stay away whether I'm sleeping good or not,* Robert thought.

He turned his face away from the door to the window. His view consisted of a nice slice of sky and some foliage. The sun was shining today, making the tree leaves a deep green. His room faced a courtyard of grass and trees between two parallel wings of the hospital. He'd been out there occasionally. It was a mini park for invalid patients with a meandering sidewalk meant to keep you moving, if slowly. Riding in a chair made him dizzy as the orderly pushed him along the many s-curves in the path. Walking it with his crutches or a walker was worse. He was just learning to walk in straight lines, and the constant shifting of his weight from side to side along the curves was hell.

He went inside himself mentally to do a pain inventory. His left leg was still a laundry list of hurts in general, but when he could focus, Robert could separate the one big pain stemming from the bone fragments knitting together from the many other pains radiating from the numerous sores, cuts, and burns from his knee to toes.

The Renatas had started breaking bones in his left foot, starting with the toes. Then they then burned their way up to the knee. He could still hear one brother (he couldn't tell which it was) tell the unidentified captain wielding the industrial soldering iron to keep making burns up his leg. "Don't stop 'til you burn his balls off." The brother had explained that when they reached his penis and balls, they'd move from his left leg to his right arm at the fingers, and keep going until they reached his collarbone. If he was still alive at that point, they would repeat with the right leg and left arm before he got a bullet in the forehead.

The brothers had worked on Robert and Alan for at least two hours, from what the FBI rescue team could determine. Robert had lost all track of time by the time his third toe was broken. Then the brothers started working on him and his partner in turns.

"Damn, why did Alan break first? He had a wife and two little boys. I should have gone first." Robert's shrink continued to tell him to let that guilt go, but Robert couldn't. One day he hoped he could exorcise it—the shrink called it something like Survivor Guilt, but who knows.

The Renatas shifted focus entirely to Alan once he started babbling. Robert's nightmares often focused on that moment. He'd been lying on the concrete, praying for unconsciousness, even though he knew that meant a bullet, just to stop the waves of pain. When Alan lost control of bodily functions and broke down for a minute, the torturer took a sledgehammer and smashed it into the middle of Robert's thigh. They knew Alan's worry over his partner overrode his personal concerns. When the torturer raised the hammer over Robert's head, Alan regained some control and begged him not to do it. From that point on Alan fed them what they wanted to know, doing his best to skirt or obscure any details he gave to protect the investigation as best as he could.

When the sledge came down, Robert heard his femur crunch and felt the bone shatter. The resulting waves of pain finally took him under. His last coherent thought was a prayer that Alan could keep up the slight aberrations in his stories. Then Robert turned his life and Alan's over to God and passed out.

The rescue team pieced together the rest. The FBI had bugged Sparky as part of the investigation, and heard something about the grocery store. Prior recon had indicated that the Renata's grocery store was the prime spot they used to torture traitors. If needed, they could use the butcher shop saws to disembody corpses, but mostly they would just use the dumpsters. The sour smell of rotten produce and expired meat easily hid the smell of decomposing flesh, and the garbage trucks on that route were part of their racket. They could also use the big freezers to freeze a body for a time, and then transport it later when things cooled down.

The FBI team monitoring Alan and Robert had flagged 'Grocery Store' as a trouble phrase, and when Robert and Alan were overdue for their nightly check-in, and were not found in their usual haunts and the monitors heard this phrase, the team set out for the store hoping to rescue the agents.

No one knows for sure how long Robert was unconscious, or how long Alan's torture continued after Robert passed out, but the FBI prepared a timeline based on what the entry teams encountered. Team Two's members preparing to break in the front door heard the shot that killed Alan. The shot mobilized both the front and back door teams. By the time the agents coming in the front of the store reached the back of the store, Team One had exchanged fire with the mobsters. Both Renata brothers at the store and the torturer were dead. Sparky was critically injured and didn't make it through surgery. Robert had second and third degree burns up his left leg. Most of the bones were broken in his left foot, his left thigh was crushed, and his hands and face were covered with contusions and bruises from his capture. Alan was worse. The burns had reached his groin and his right hand was crushed. They had shot him through the jaw, severing the arteries in his neck, and it wasn't clear whether he bled out or drowned in blood. The shot to his jaw was one of the ways the Renatas signaled victory—that he'd talked.

The operation was considered a qualified success. Despite the torture and beatings of their agents, both Robert and Alan had microchip recorders in their clothes and on their bodies. The recorders caught all the audio and the Renatas addressed everyone in the back room by known aliases. When the Renatas searched the agents, they had not found the recorder in Robert's shaggy hair, nor the one embedded in Alan's shoe.

After the incident, Robert was hospitalized for months. The worst burns healed with the aid of skin grafts, but he had large chunks of flesh missing all along his leg. The doctors were able to re-structure his foot and pin everything back together. For some reason most of the foot fractures were clean breaks. His thigh was another story. The tissues compartmentalized, and the femur was crushed. Many surgeries, pins, and transplants of donor bone and tissue helped rebuild his thigh. The doctors worked diligently to save the leg and at times worried that the burns would become infected or the donor bone would be rejected, either situation would require amputation. The doctors aimed for a recovery where 'you'll walk again.' Everyone determined that to have Robert run, jump, etc. was too high a goal.

Chapter Three
Reva Has a Bad Day

"I can't do this anymore." Reva half-sobbed. Hearing herself speak the words against her will horrified Reva. She never lost control like this. Never. Not when her grandpa died, or even when her partner, Carl was killed. "Why now? What's so different about being thirty-eight?" It was dark in her spacious living room. She hadn't had a chance to put up blinds in her new condo, let alone pick curtains and the bare glass let in the lights of the city and what moonlight could get through the trees bordering the property. The naked windows made Reva feel exposed and worried.

Years of training and FBI operations had made Reva paranoid. She *knew* how easy it was for someone to spy on her through the unobstructed windows, especially if she had her lights on. She'd come home with groceries and stashed them in the ultra-modern kitchen with its granite counters, glass-tile backsplash, and sleek, steel appliances by the light of the enormous fridge. Her two measly bags of groceries looked pathetic in the bright white cavern of her new fridge. The glass shelves practically sparkled at her like the pendant lights with their crystal covers dangling over the bar.

"I'm crazy for buying this place." She said out loud, then thought, "Great, now I'm talking to myself, like Jenny does. Damn her." Looking at the pretty view of the river out the eight-foot high window in her great room, she felt the tears come. "I'm lonely." The thought came unbidden and unwanted. Her mother had tried to warn her. Her pal Jenny had sensed it, but now Reva felt the depressing thought rush over her.

Reva had joined the FBI at age twenty, the minute she'd graduated college. Her good grades had graced her with the honor of graduating high school at seventeen. It seemed her whole life centered around the FBI for almost twenty years. Not only was tomorrow her thirty-eighth birthday, it was also her eighteen-year anniversary of service in the FBI. What did she have to show for this, she wondered.

It's only the aftermath after today's incident, stop beating yourself up. Even Stan confirmed Flanagan deserved it. Recriminations overwhelmed Reva, so she sat in the dark on the plush carpet in front of her new condo's picture window and began meditating in the lotus position.

Carefully Reva began thinking about her day. While part of her concentrated on her breathing and aligning her chakras, the rest of her brain systematically reviewed the incident that was upsetting her.

As the main female fight instructor in her DC FBI office, Reva taught daily hand-to-hand combat classes. Sometimes the classes were to help female agents learn techniques they could use to overcome opponents, especially opponents who were larger and heavier than them, but most of her classes were mixed-gender, and served to toughen up any agent. Each year, Reva was given some of the trouble-children from the FBI recruiters to see if she could fix their problems. Mostly she worked with agents struggling with fighting techniques, but sometimes the top brass would send her men who had issues with 'females'. Some of them couldn't hit a woman, some out of fear of hurting them, others due to a respect of females, or other baggage from their upbringing, and since Reva was in top condition and used to taking hits, she served to help them get over this hurdle. Other agents felt that females should not be in law enforcement, and Reva was often tasked show them that a woman could handle the physical aspects of the job. In any case, Reva proved her competence with what her buddies termed her 'mad skills'.

But, sometimes, she received male recruits who hid their negative issues at first. That was the situation with

Flanagan. He'd passed the psych tests and seemed okay, but he'd gotten mouthy with one of the female analysts giving him training. His supervisor called him out for it, and though Flanagan later apologized and he had been a model student ever since, some of the other trainees noticed some passive/aggressive behavior between Flanagan and the analyst. One of the other trainees had even told the supervisor, that Flanagan had issues with the female recruits. To test him, the top brass planted a younger-looking senior female agent in his classes to observe him, and over time she confirmed that Flanagan seemed biased against females; he thought them inferior, and figured in general they were only there because they were sleeping with somebody.

His supervisors wanted to know how deep Flanagan's resentment ran, so they warned Reva and then put Flanagan in her advanced combat class. Reva taught the class to any agents or recruits who had the basics down pat. She'd do this in six-week sessions for five days a week, and had done the current class for about three weeks when Flanagan was brought in. She had built a rapport with this latest group, and one of her good buddies, Jock was repeating the class for fun and had agreed to be her sparring partner for this go-round.

You know Flanagan was primed and ready for it. He was all puffed up and cocky after the last instructor had told him he was too good for the basics and elevated him here. He had no idea this was a plant... Flanagan was too cocky to even wonder why this invitation came out of the blue. Reva reviewed the past few days leading up to today. Flanagan had taken stock of the other students and had held his own, though it was work for him. By day three, yesterday, he was sure of himself and had quit worrying about his performance. He didn't know that the other students were being soft on him, but he was earning their respect because he *was* improving. Today Flanagan had been clearly happy to be there and excited to learn a new technique. He'd even made a few friends and was accepted by the group.

As they finished their warm-ups, Reva caught Jock's eye and nodded. That was their signal. Today they would push Flanagan and see what happened. By now, Flanagan had observed the class's respect for Reva and knew that only the best were asked to spar with her. Reva suspected he believed that because Jock was her buddy, he was taking it easy on her—and so Reva and Jock plotted to get Flanagan's beliefs out in the open.

Reva clapped her hands once, loudly, to get the class's attention. Jock stood to her right. "Ok guys, now we're going to show you my favorite roundhouse kick so you can practice it and get your speed up. Remember learning to do roundhouses takes time, and your opponent will be able to predict your actions and get you off guard if you're not careful."

She gestured to Jock, who spun around superfast and raised his leg trying to kick Reva in the head. He was quick, and being six-inches taller, everyone expected her to get knocked out. Reva was faster, and with the ease of long-practice she watched Jock out of the corner of her eye. By the time his foot was coming at her she'd turned towards him, and blocked his leg up with the side of her left arm to knock him off balance as she simultaneously dropped to one knee in a crouch at his waist. She popped back up and spoke as Jock regained his stance. "Another way works like this." Reva spun the other direction and aimed her kick at Jock's chest. He was just as fast in his reaction, but instead of knocking her leg up and away he turned, crouched slightly and spun into her kick, grabbing her leg. At this point, they both froze. "From here, you've got to be good at being one-legged and need to prepare yourself for a hell of a fracture." Jock gestured with his arms holding her leg and calmly showed how he could damage Reva's ankle, knee, and thigh depending on his grip, etc. Reva continued her instruction narrating Jock's actions, "You don't want the groin injury that will put you on the ground either." With that Jock twisted and forced Reva to twist with him and land on her back at his feet. "Notice he still has my leg and can easily pull out the gun and finish me. Remember Rule #1, people: Never let them get you on the ground."

Reva carefully demonstrated all aspects of the kick again and set the class to practicing. She wandered amidst the group. They looked like ballet dancers standing on one leg and spinning. She worked to correct form as needed, and at the half-hour mark demonstrated how to kick with the other leg, then set the class to practice that.

"Ok everyone, good work. Remember you don't have to live your fighting life left or right-handed, or left or right-legged. Use your whole body and practice with both…You want to be just as lethal with the other hand folks." Reva winked, and the veterans all laughed with her. They all fought like classic swordsmen—using their weaker side more than their strong side, to keep both sides lethal.

A knock sounded at the door. Reva walked over to open it. "Ok, everyone, we have an hour left, in which you are going to work on maintaining control with your speed and putting your power into those kicks. Here are today's volunteers. With that, twenty FBI agents in full protective gear filed past Reva into the room. Each moved until they were paired with one of the classmates. Reva looked to Jock, who nodded as he buckled on his chest pads. They both glanced over to Flanagan, where one of the best female FBI fighters, Hannah stood next to him. Reva heard Jock quietly remark, "I wonder how our poster boy will like taking a few kicks at Amazon woman." Reva smiled in reply, as she gave the final instructions. "Ok folks. Our volunteers have all stood where you are. As you can see, they came prepared, and can take whatever you dish out. For the next twenty minutes, practice kicking with your good leg and start with form, then see how fast you can go, and then work on power. Begin."

To reassure a few folks who were hesitating, Reva motioned Jock over, "Don't worry about hurting these guys. This gear works." Reva then kicked Jock three times clockwise, then twice counter-clockwise, and then three more times using her other leg in quick succession. She aimed all her kicks for the same spot on Jock's mid section. When she was done she motioned to Jock, who stripped off his chest and body pads, and lifted his T-shirt to show the side. "See, a little redness, but no big marks or welts. Our volunteers may feel a bit banged up after, but they're used to this kind of punishment - and it will serve to toughen their bodies." Reva bent down and helped Jock stash his pads, and they began wandering amongst the trainees. Reva hovered near Flanagan, while Jock stood nearby as they observed him.

Unlike some of the other fighters, Flanagan was quiet as he practiced. He breathed deeply, but did not vocalize or shout as he kicked, instead he grunted. Reva observed him. Over time, Flanagan's form and control improved, and she could tell he was really getting into it. Reva glanced up to Hannah, who winked. *Ok. Hannah's okay, and Flanagan is staying in bounds.* As she watched she could almost hear Flanagan thinking, "Go down, dammit. Go DOWN!" Reva watched and bided her time. *Yup, sure enough, he's forgetting form in his quest to get her down.*

Reva had speculated that Flanagan would not be able the resist a chance to beat the crap out of a female fighter. She and Jock had discussed whom to use at length, and she was glad they'd picked Hannah, who was a six-foot tall, Scandinavian Blonde beauty. She clearly had Viking genetics. Her bones were strong and thick and, though she carried no extra weight, she was honed and fit. The group liked to joke that fighting Hannah was fighting sticks and rocks, her body was so tough. Hannah had been prepared for Flanagan to lose his temper, and after the next kick looked to Reva, who winked at her, giving the signal to test him.

With that Hannah turned back to Flanagan and smiled wide as if to jeer at him. Flanagan clearly didn't like it. He was a little winded but determined. The next time he kicked at Hannah, he started a little wild, and Hannah caught his leg mid-swing and threw him to the floor at her feet. She looked down to Flanagan, and then looked over to Reva who said;

"That's' enough, Hannah, thank you." Hannah walked out of the workout room.

Reva moved in and stood over Flanagan considering him. She offered him her hand, "You want a hand up?"

Like a two-year old in a tantrum, Flanagan leaned away from her and shot back, "I'm fine!"

Reva held her hands up to show she wasn't threatening him, and stepped back. Jock joined her and they waited for Flanagan to get off the floor. Reva glanced around. The veterans were ignoring them, having been appraised of Flanagan's situation. A couple of his buddies looked concerned, but when they met Reva's eye, they returned to sparring.

Flanagan made it to his feet and was clearly pissed. Here was his moment to bear up or break down. Reva spoke again, "Mr. Flanagan, do you understand what happened?"

"Yeah, that bitch stopped sparring and took me down."

Reva cut him off, "No, you got emotional and lost your temper, forgot your form, and went after your opponent, who kept her head and took you down to give you a chance to cool off."

Reva forced Flanagan to look her in the eye. She was glad he was slightly taller than her; she enjoyed how she tried to stare her down. "Can you calm yourself?" She asked in her softest, sweetest voice, then waited. Flanagan was clearly upset but composed himself. Reva caught him looking to the left and right, checking to see if others were observing his humiliation. No one was overtly watching them. He then looked up over Reva's shoulder at Jock and then met Reva's calm stare. "Yes, Ma'am, I'm calm."

"Good. I was told, when they put you in my class, that you have a problem with female FBI agents." Reva spoke quietly, and she could tell she'd shocked Flanagan. "I believe that while there are differences between the sexes, each of us must work to overcome any weaknesses that are born within us, that regardless of gender. *Any* FBI agent can overcome their handicaps in order to excel at their duties." Reva looked at Flanagan, "Consider this a safe environment, Mr. Flanagan. I'd like to hear your thoughts."

Flanagan looked away, clearly deciding whether to speak or hold his peace. He turned back, looked at Jock and Reva. "Look. I don't think women should be FBI agents. They don't make good police, nor should they be in the military." He waited a minute. Reva stayed quiet, wanting him to vent. "Ok. Fine. I am not saying they need to be barefoot and pregnant, but I don't think a woman can protect my back when the chips are down, okay?"

Reva answered clearly, knowing that the others would be listening for her response, while pretending to ignore them. "I understand. However, have you ever served with or observed a woman performing in combat or a tense situation? Have you any empirical evidence to support your beliefs?"

"Well no, but you know. Girls are softer; they can't take as much as we can. They get hurt easier and don't have as much power."

"I see. Well Mr. Flanagan, I think you need to consider doubting your premises. In the meantime, I'd like you to think about your .45, and whether my reflexes would be faster than yours in a firefight." Before Flanagan could respond, Reva delivered a roundhouse kick that knocked him on his ass. She stood over him, finishing her lecture, "That probably hurt. Flanagan, know this: you were put in my class purposely so the brass could see whether or not you have a problem with female FBI agents. As the FBI will not reverse its policy of recruiting more female agents, you need to accept this fact. As you work on this issue consider that two females, both shorter and smaller than you, have placed you on your ass today. I can take you down any day and any time I choose, even if you're ready for me to attack. That's a fact. Until you have the years of training I do in hand-to-hand combat, you will have a hard time taking me down, despite outweighing me and being male."

Reva's temper began to come through and her words hardened. "It's my *job* to take down bad-asses who are bigger, taller, and maybe tougher than me, and out to kill me or worse. I work hard so that I am able to do this. I excel at hand-to-hand combat, so I help others learn these skills, regardless of gender. You have a problem, Mr. Flanagan, but if you can overcome it I think you'll make an outstanding FBI agent." With that, Reva was done. She looked around the class, and announced. "Class is over for today." and walked out of the room.

As she left, she heard Jock remark to Flanagan, as he helped him up. "They recorded us on the short circuit T.V. I suggest you stop by your supervisor's office once you have cleaned up."

As she relived these events, Reva felt the same anger again and let it wash over her and dissipate finally. Before she'd left work today, her supervisor Stan called her into his office and she and Jock watched the tape with him.

Afterward, Stan commented, "I see that you lost your temper, but you remained professional. We supervisors agreed that you were right to take him down with a kick without padding, because it seemed to sink in. It looked like you got Flanagan's attention."

Jock interrupted when Reva glanced to him during Stan's statement, "I agree. She should have kicked him. A little physical pain should help him overcome his bias."

Stan smiled and nodded, "Good." He looked back to Reva, "We're in consensus. You made the right call. Don't let it get to you, he needed proof and I can tell you held back and didn't serve him the full Reva power. Good work. Flanagan will speak to a counselor about his bias as he continues the training, and his supervisor has hopes we can move him past it. Ironically, when his boss asked him whether a female could be a dangerous criminal, that really got Flanagan's attention and he realized his prejudice could put him in danger. This incident seems to have been a break-through for him. So, Reva, you saved a good agent from one hell of a blind spot. Thanks."

Reva focused on that approbation and let it wash over her. Finally she could work through her emotions so she could move on to tomorrow. She needed a fresh take on her job before she faced her birthday. Thirty-eight years old. Eighteen years with the FBI. Reva sighed.

Chapter Four
Robert's Rehab

Grant, Robert's supervisor was briefing the other DC supervisors on his status, "Well, Robert Leland survived the latest surgery and it looks like he's going to make it. I can't pin the doctors down on any specifics, but it's clear he'll walk again, but he'll have limits with the leg. We have no proof yet, but reports show the Renatas are going to come after him, but we don't have any specifics at this time, so we're leaving security as is for now."

Grant cleared his throat and continued, "I'm concerned over how to proceed with his career. You know that he's always been one of my best under-covers with the mob cases, but the doctors are fairly certain that while he will be able to walk, running will be impossible. I could wait a year for rehabilitation if I knew I could get seventy-five percent of my agent back, but it's more like he'll only get to fifty percent of his prior form, and I worry he won't suit if he can't be a bad ass for a mobster. Does anyone have any openings?"

The supervisors looked around the room, each weighing Robert's past stellar performance along with his new limits. Stan Hammond, Reva's FBI supervisor, had worked with Robert back closer to his rookie days, and spoke up,

"You all know that I was Robert's boss when he first came to DC. My group needs a lot of desk support and analysis, and I think that Robert could pair well with Reva on her few undercover assignments. I don't believe a limp or even a wheelchair would hinder the kind of work Reva does—as she's usually on deep-recon. For the rest of the time, Robert can do deskwork while she's in the gym teaching classes—He has a fine mind and eye for detail."

Stan looked around the large leather padded conference table, "Does anyone have any other or better options? Does anyone dispute me taking Robert into my unit?" A few of the others shook their heads and then nodded their agreement.

Grant smiled. "Stan, that's a great idea, plus it fixes problems for both of us. None of us have been able to find a suitable partner for Reva. Both she and Robert have similar years of service and experience, and may work out great. Let's do it." Positive noises echoed Grant's words as continued. "I'll make the transfer effective next pay period."

Stan interjected, "So, we'll make it a straight-forward transfer, your team to mine, and I'll take care of the disability paper work from today on." Grant nodded. Stan made a notation in his PDA and closed the cover to emphasize the close of the deal. "I'll tell Robert about the transfer when I go see him tomorrow." He accepted Robert's medical file from Grant and called his secretary, Denise to clear his morning schedule.

***

Robert lay flat on his back on the therapy table reading the FBI memo his morning nurse had brought. While the therapist checked the mobility in his leg, Robert read that he was moving to a new FBI team and that his old boss, Stan, would become his new boss sometime next week.

Stan had come to see him ever since he'd made it through the first surgery. Robert smiled ignoring the pain in his leg as he felt hope for the first time in these past weeks. He could return to the FBI after all this. With this hope, maybe he could endure his recovery.

Over these past months, twice Robert's body went septic due to infections in his leg. Three times, he went 'crazy' when a procedure pushed him past his limits and he'd had to be sedated in order to heal. The doctors considered inducing him into a coma, but Stan said no. Instead he put the best FBI psychologists on the case. He hoped to recover his agent with the most skills possible. Stan admired Robert and hoped he could return to the 'land of the living' at least.

Robert prayed again, "Thank you, God, once again for putting me in Stan's hands." Grant had placed him on indefinite disability, of course. In Robert's mind it seemed clear that Grant was all for retiring him out of the FBI on full disability, while Stan seemed to want him recovered and back in the FBI. Robert knew Stan had kept tabs on him through the years. *Whatever the reason, I am glad Stan stepped in. He knows how Grant and I don't get along.* Robert had chosen to move back to DC from Dallas after his divorce partly so he could speak to Stan more often.

Robert thought about his life for a minute. He knew Stan thought his relationship with Grant was toxic because of his own self-destructive behavior after the divorce. He could admit now that he'd purposely distanced himself from his family when he refused to move back home to Colorado and choosing DC instead. So here he lay, recently divorced, with a career on hold, and having lost his partner. As he thought, Robert realized that Stan was now the only person left in the DC office that he knew well and got along with.

As weeks passed Stan became Robert's support, and he did it both as a boss, and friend. He helped Robert transition to his FBI terrorism team from his past mob activities unit. Robert appreciated Stan's confidence in him. He acted like he knew he could do the job. Stan vowed to be there for him, even if he ended up crippled—mentally, physically or both. Stan spoke of a real future, and didn't use phrases like 'we're retiring you' or 'we'll see what happens.'

Stan began coming by to see Robert a couple of times a week with small or old case files. He'd remarked once, "I'm going to use your brain until I can use your body too." He brought in an FBI laptop and had a team give Robert appropriate security. He then worked with the FBI psychologists to come up with an algorithm to time his visits. He wanted to be there often enough that Robert would began to expect them, but random enough that they wouldn't become routine. The shrink confirmed whenever Robert formed a routine, his thoughts would descend into depressed chaos by the third or fourth day. Stan was determined to keep Robert busy, but not overload him, and give him just enough structure that he could plan a little.

One thing Stan did consistently was to spend Sunday mornings talking with Robert about God and spiritual matters. He worked to tap into Robert's childhood past of regular Sunday church attendance to take Robert back emotionally to a place before he was FBI, had married his ex, and was tortured. He and the doctors hoped that he could keep Robert's emotions in a good place as he healed physically, and then everyone would help him deal with his emotional trauma over the torture. The plan started to work. Robert worked on the FBI stuff as he could and it gave him something productive to do. He even helped solve a couple of cases. He also looked forward to Sundays, and began happily expecting Stan's visits as they could happen any day. Anticipation helped him find contentment in small things, and Robert finally began to feel at peace as often as he felt out of control.

At six months out, Stan started inviting various people he knew to visit Robert on Sunday afternoons. This added more positive social interaction to Robert's life. He introduced it by saying, "Robert, the team really appreciates the work you've done. They see your name all the time but most haven't met you. Now that your infections are cleared up, could I bring one or two in to meet you tomorrow afternoon?"

These additional visits worked to further improve Robert's moods. Robert had always moved around in the FBI and was a people person. He'd always done well integrating into a new team, and so the weekly visits of his team members and others really helped him connect with new people. They started talking work, and then progressed to talking life, and Robert made new friends for the first time since moving to DC.

At nine months out, Robert relapsed. By then the remaining, known members of the Renata organization were finally coming under indictment, and the Justice Department guys were starting to prep him in case he needed to testify. They leveled with him about how showing his wounds would help the jury see the reality of what the brothers did to those who crossed them, but Robert had little interest in being on display.

The decision was made for them when his body began to reject part of the cadaver bone in his thigh. More surgery was required, so Robert was unable to testify at the first trial. Then someone tried to kill him in the hospital.

Chapter Five
Lavender

Robert lay on the gurney, blinked and looked around trying to get his bearings. He remembered being wheeled down the hall for this surgery. His last conscious memory was the doctor telling what she was going to do, and the anesthesia knocking him out mid-explanation.

Robert felt like he was swaying, though he knew he was lying down. He hated how he could come out of the anesthesia so fast. At this stage, the pain would come back and the staff could do nothing until the residual anesthetic had cleared his system. He tried to relax and force himself to sleep. *Damn. Every time I have to lay here for hours until they wheel me back to the room and finally knock me out so I can sleep through the pain.*

He sighed raggedly, and had nearly drifted off to sleep, when he heard a scuffed step near the room's door. The recovery room was only partially lit, so Robert could only see the outline of a man in scrubs, and he didn't recognize him. Besides, when the staff came for him after surgeries, they turned on the lights first. His warning system went off.

At first he was shocked. Robert's internal radar had not gone off like this since the incident. Maybe he was having a nightmare. Here he was lying while the same horrific fear of death came over him from his dreams. *I am awake, so this must be real!* Cold sweat broke out on his forehead and under his arms. *I'm naked on a gurney with my left leg bandaged and bundled up from surgery. I could throw my blankets over him, but I can barely move.* Robert tried desperately to think of a way to protect himself as the man came closer. Robert prayed, and a thought came to him. Stan insisted he have a panic or trouble buzzer like the medic alert bracelets older folks use when they are alone— to call for help when they cannot move or speak. He knew

Stan meant him to use it when a panic attack came, but he used it now. Half-closing his eyes he pretended to be unconscious as the orderly reached his side. His right arm was lying on his chest directly over the buzzer the staff had placed on a chain around his neck. Praying that the intruder wouldn't see his thumb, Robert's Boy Scout training kicked in. He pushed three short 'dit, dit, dit' pulses then three longer 'dot, dot, dot' pulses and then three short 'dit, dit, dit' pulses on the buzzer hoping he was remembering the Morse code for SOS. Robert kept repeating the pulses as he watched the orderly stop just out of reach at his IV tree. Robert calculated the distance, and determined that there was no way four feet off the ground and two feet away that he could reach the man in his current state. He kept sending his distress message, praying someone would hear. Horror flooded him as he watched the orderly inject something into his saline drip. The man glanced at him, pocketed the syringe and left.

Robert stared after the stranger and watched the IV fluids flowing into his left arm. He felt weakness coming over him, but it was the tightening in the back of his throat that told him he would die of anaphylaxis—allergic shock. Robert imagined he felt the tissues in his throat swell and grow hives as he lost consciousness.

He didn't know he'd muttered, "I bet it was lavender," before he lost consciousness. Robert also didn't know that two nurses had rushed into the room and heard him as he went under. They'd heard his buzzer, but didn't see the man leave.

The killer knew what he was doing. Robert was allergic to lavender. Whenever he touched it he'd break out in hives and develop rashes. This wasn't a problem in the hospital, because the staff knew of his severe allergy and ensured nothing containing lavender oil, essence or extract was used near him or in his room.

***

"Thank heavens the hospital was prepared for anaphylactic shock and had everything on hand to save him." Stan remarked as he stood over Robert's bed a few hours later. He turned to his second-in-command Reva and said, "I need you here. Full-time, personal protection from here on. The Renatas aren't going anywhere soon, and we'll need to watch over Robert until we can move him to Denver. I don't think you guys will get to be partners after all."

Reva, nodded.

Chapter Six
Robert, Meet Reva

Robert woke up and felt like carpet lined his throat and mouth. He spoke aloud to what he thought was an empty room. "Damn, I'd kill for a cold Dr. Pepper." A female voice startled him,

"No good. That won't help the phlegm. Straight water, or maybe some herbal tea with honey?"

Robert turned his head to look at where the voice was coming from on his right.

She was medium tall, he'd guess about five-foot-six, maybe taller, but he couldn't tell as she was leaning against the windowsill. The afternoon sun shone down on him and backlit the woman, showing a lithe but curved silhouette while highlighting the curly hairs around her head.

She straightened up and walked the two steps to stand right next to the bed. Maybe it was the sudden appearance of her face from shadow into sun, but Robert's life changed in that moment. The woman had healthy golden skin and a few freckles, but also the most beautiful heart-shaped face he'd ever seen up close. Dark brows and eyelashes accentuated her multi-colored, mostly golden-brown and green eyes, a perfect nose, and full dark-pink lips. She came closer and Robert saw her hair, which just looked brown at first, was actually a reddish-brown mix of colors. She smiled and his heart fluttered.

"Hello, Robert. I'm Reva—Stan's second in command or chief gopher." She reached out and clasped his right hand, squeezing it in lieu of making him raise it to shake hands. She moved back and cocked her head, obviously studying him.

Robert's mouth recovered faster than his heart did, allowing him to make small talk. "Yea, the others told me about you, you aren't around on Sundays…something about weekend car rides?" Robert recalled that Reva, being Jewish, started her Sabbath on Friday evening and kept it through Saturday evening, but would spend Sundays driving around in her classic car. He thought that he should remember the kind she drove, but that fact escaped him at the moment as he stared at her.

Reva smiled and looked around the room as she chatted, "You heard right. I spend every Sunday driving somewhere—mostly to exercise my baby, but also to just explore. I am a bit of a foodie, so I like to try different restaurants when I can. But mostly I like to see new places, especially ones with local or historical interest – that kind of thing."

When she paused, Robert asked, "Baby? I thought you weren't married."

Reva laughed. "Good way to segue in to asking whether I'm married or not. Just kidding, I know what you meant. My *baby* is my '73 Chevelle. I've had her since I was twenty-five. At first, I just maintained her, but over time, maintenance became restoration. I've done everything to her, some things a couple of times. I put a new Chevy 350 in her about six years ago, and have racked up 150,000 miles on it and hope to get to 300,000 before I am done."

"Wow!" Robert said as he tried to assimilate Reva's car craziness with what he had heard about her. *I like this woman. Let's see if she'll stay here and chat with me. I knew she had to be good to be Stan's second, but she proved it by not answering whether she's married or not, though I don't see a ring.*

Reva continued, "I didn't come here to talk cars, although I could do that for hours whenever you like. I came here to get to know you. How *are* you? We nearly lost you there."

Robert paused, taken aback. "What day is it?"

"Wednesday." Reva answered.

"Then I don't know how I am. The last thing I

remember was on Sunday night watching some guy inject poison into my IV, and then I was waking up feeling warm because the sun was cooking my right side right before I saw you." Robert faltered, and looked a little lost.

Reva came over to him. "Oh God. I am so sorry Robert. I thought Stan had briefed you already. Hasn't anyone come to see you yet?" Reva didn't give him a chance to respond, but moved over to the door and opened it. Robert overheard her, "Caspar, call Stan. Robert's awake and ready for debriefing."

He heard a male voice answer her. It sounded familiar, but he couldn't be sure. There was a Caspar on Stan's team but he couldn't remember meeting him. Reva came back over. "I'll be right back. I came in to see if you were up, and when I saw you sleeping but moving your hand, I figured you'd come out of the coma and already seen the doctors and Stan. Let me check with the staff. While I am out, I'll get you a drink and be back in a jiff to fill you in."

Reva came back a little later with a paper bag and an insulated hospital mug full of ice water, accompanied by Robert's regular day nurse. The nurse rushed over to his monitors, and checked his stats. As she made some notations in the computer, she remarked, "Mr. Leland, I am so sorry. The doctors changed your meds to allow you to come out of the coma today, but they didn't expect you to wake up until later. I don't know why the machines didn't go off." She looked down and saw that one of the electrodes had come loose. Plugging it back in, she continued, "You're early as usual, but your vitals look good, I'm just going to get Dr. Qalat to come see you."

Reva asked, "Is it okay for me to give him a drink?"

"Oh sure, he's fine—no food yet, but any liquids should be fine." The nurse answered and left. As she opened the door, Robert and Reva heard her speak into the radio, "Get Qal down here. Yea. Leland's awake. The left cord came loose."

Reva pulled Robert's hospital table over and deposited her bag and the mug on it. "Can I help you sit up?" She asked.

"No, no-no. I got it, if I can find the blasted control." Robert tried to move his hands around as best he could, but he couldn't feel the bed remote or its tethered cord on either side.

Reva came over and stood near his head. She leaned over him and reached to the shelf above his head. "Here it is." She stood straight to hand him the remote after showing it above his head so he could see it and reach it.

Robert concentrated on grabbing it properly so he could hold the control in his right hand without dropping it. *Oh my heavens, she smells like sunshine and sin and woman.* He thought trying to regain control of himself. He'd stared at the soft curve of her breast as Reva leaned over him and he could smell her perfume. Reva moved back and tugged the hospital table over by her, so Robert could sit up.

***

Reva watched as Robert's bed sat him up. He paused at about twenty degrees and stated, "I always pause a few times to keep from being dizzy when I've been down for a while. How long was I out, anyway?"

"Oh, just since Sunday. So what, three or four days? Stan told me they stopped the allergic reaction with epinephrine and industrial strength antihistamines, but it was touch and go for a few hours. Once your body settled down, they chose to put you in a coma for a while, to keep things calm and to allow your stitches to heal. I guess that first night, you tossed and turned and thrashed around something terrible. They gave up and sedated you, and then your blood pressure tanked. From what I hear they called you 'trouble' for a while. Stan told me they started the process to bring you out of the coma last night, and they expected you awake today sometime."

Robert's response was brief "Wow."

"Hey man, I understand. It's a lot to take in. I'll hang out while you assimilate data." Reva turned around and quietly looked out the window for a few minutes.

Reva heard the bed motor raising Robert two more times before she turned back. She'd known his statistics, but seeing his six-foot, two-inch and ex-football player, now honed FBI agent physique up close was astounding. He was sitting up now and looking at her with interest. He was tall enough that he sat taller than she where she stood and she had to look up to meet his eyes. Even in a hospital gown his shoulders looked broad and strong. She was impressed that he'd kept up his upper body strength and her mouth went dry looking at his arm muscles.

Stan wants you to be partners eventually, don't get distracted by his sexiness. Rein it in. Reva told herself silently—she just met Robert, it this was no time to get overheated over his looks. She spoke to cover her flustered state, "I suppose when the doctor gets here, he'll fill you in."

Robert interrupted, "Dr. Qalat is a girl. She's been working on me as long as I've been here and she's done most of my surgeries. She's from Pakistan and very nice, as well as competent."

"That's neat. Hm. I guess as a female FBI agent, I should have allowed for your doctor to be female and not said 'him' automatically." Reva chuckled and was thoughtful for a moment, then continued her narrative, "Anyway, the staff heard your SOSs and hurried to your recovery room. I guess the day shift nurses knew you have a habit of coming out of anesthesia quickly, but someone forgot to tell the night shift in their rush to get you in. They had worried that you had fallen or something, but when they got to you, your color wasn't good. The nurses heard you say something about lavender and then you passed out.

Thankfully, they considered anaphylaxis along with cardiac arrest and saved you."

Reva moved closer and motioned to his neck, "I don't know if you noticed, but they had to do a tracheotomy on you." She stared at Robert's neck and watched him jerk and then slowly move his hand to his neck and feel the bandage.

Robert asked, "I guess I was breathing okay and they took out the breathing tube?"

Reva nodded. "Stan asked if I could come by early today and see how you were as he had some briefings he couldn't miss." She turned away to get the hospital table. Once it was maneuvered within Robert's reach she nudged the hospital mug to him. "Here's some cool ice water. It should help with the phlegm etc." Reva reached into the brown paper bag as she continued, "The guys told me you loved Dr. Pepper, and that the hospital only had Coke, so I stopped by the store and got you a supply." Reva pulled out four 2-liter bottles of Dr. Pepper. She looked around. "Stan said they had given you a nice set-up here with a mini fridge?"

"Yes, they've made my room as homey as possible. It's over there under the cabinet by the closet."

Reva followed Robert's gaze and spotted it. She toted the Dr. Pepper over, and looked back over her shoulder to ask, "Can I get you some now? I can go fetch some ice and another mug." She didn't wait for him to reply but bent down to the fridge and put the bottles in.

***

Robert enjoyed the view as Reva bent over. *Damn, and a fine ass in those jeans too. I'm in trouble.* He sighed.

Reva must have heard it, because she turned back. "So, a Pepper?"

He smiled. Reva referred to a Dr. Pepper drink as a 'Pepper' just like his mom used to when he was young. "No, no, the water's great thanks." Robert thought for a second and decided on a plan to spend as much time with her as possible. "Hey, there's a chair over there, pull it over here and sit and talk with me until the doctor gets here. You might as well debrief me. We got to 'they gave me a tracheotomy'."

Reva smiled, lighting up her face, and complied. "So, after they got you stable, the staff examined you to see how the allergen got into your system. They couldn't find any rashes or hives for topical contact, and then checked you for injection sites. They also wondered whether someone injected something into your IV lines. Stan had said that that's what he would do—impersonate a hospital worker and get you through the IV. The bag tested negative, but the line showed traces of lavender extract. Meanwhile we were rushing to interview staff—Stan called in a team that night—and we reviewed all the surveillance tapes we could." Reva stretched her long legs away from the chair and looked at him. He smiled at her and nodded, so she continued. "Well, we spotted someone come in from the patient parking lot in scrubs. We followed him on the recordings. This guy had a badge and looked like an orderly, but he didn't check in with the desks or go into any of the staff areas. He came straight in, took the elevator to the operating floor and walked right to your recovery room. The guy smiled and nodded to everyone he saw, but cocked his head at every point where a camera could catch his face. He came out of the recovery room about two minutes later and retraced his route stopping in a rest room on the way out before he got into a non-descript gray sedan. We couldn't catch the plate in the dark… it had one of those smoky plastic covers that reflect the light for the cameras. The forensics team canvassed that restroom and found the syringe disposal container was full—it's the closest room to the dialysis section so a bunch of diabetics must use it to inject insulin. Anyway, they tested all the syringes and found one with no prints, but containing lavender extract residue. There were also traces of saline solution in the same concentration as your drip. So, we can't ID the guy or the car, but we're pretty sure the Renatas called a hit out on you. They knew how to get to you, and did so on the day before the first Renata trial. I personally think they were waiting for your next surgery to make your death look like a medical accident or mistake. I don't know whether we could have proven anaphylaxis if you hadn't have spoken. Have you had the symptoms before; do you think you recognized them?"

Robert thought for a moment. He'd woken up in the throes of a dream where someone was stalking him with lavender branches. "I clearly remember coming to, and hoping they would get me back to my room, where I could be more comfortable as I waited for the pain killing drugs. I hurt all over, but noticed an unfamiliar orderly—the guy. I was too weak to really move, but had a bad feeling. I was trying to decide how to protect myself when he stopped near me and messed with my IV. I just knew he was doing something bad. I did the SOS on the alert button, because I figured I'd fall off the gurney if I tried to move." Robert paused, clearly upset, "I did nothing, I just lay there watching him inject me and leave. I don't remember finishing the SOS. I do remember a tight feeling in my throat. I knew then that it was an allergic reaction and that it had to be lavender. It's the only thing that I am *really* allergic to. My last thought was that at least finally the pain would go away." Robert looked away at the end.

Robert saw that Reva noticed his discomfort and leaned away to give him some privacy while he recovered, and commented, "You're good you know. Training, or life?" He asked. They both did the job and he figured Reva was as FBI as he.

Reva shook her head and looked away from him. "Both, but life too. I've been there. Not as bad as you, but I've been in a hospital bed after an investigation went bad knowing that I may not get out of it without help and wondering if it had been better if I'd have been in my partner's shoes." Reva said no more.

Robert was shocked. Finally he said, "You lost a partner too?"

"Yup. Reva's voice was clipped, but she breathed deeply and went on, "There was a bomb. We were sleeping in the rooms above a 300-year-old pub in London after night shift operations. The timbers came down on us. One caught my left side. Arm was bad, Leg was broken. Carl didn't make it. No chance. Crushed his chest."

"Was it the suspect?"

"Yes. His accomplice waited until all the agents she spotted went in to our HQ before triggering the device."

"How long had you been partners?"

"Seven years; from rookies. We were a good team. Undercover, stings - you name it Carl and I did it."

Robert looked at Reva. She'd continued staring away out the window. He didn't know what to say, but settled for: "The shrink tells me that there's a plan and it was my part to live. I don't understand or like that explanation, but I don't have a better one. I'm sorry."

"Thank you."

Reva turned back to him and gave a small smile. "Actually it's been more than ten years and it's easier now. The pain never goes away really, but it doesn't hit me as often. Besides, he had two little girls and one is getting ready to graduate high school. He always called his daughters the best of him, and they will go on."

Robert considered Reva's words. "That's a good point. Alan loved his family. He knew the job could kill him, but always said he'd lived all the more off the job because of it. I'll have to think on that."

Reva nodded, then asked, "Can we change the subject? It's a beautiful sunny day, and thinking of dead partners always get me down."

Robert laughed. "I agree. I like your style, lady. I never thought of consciously changing the subject."

Robert and Reva talked until Dr. Qalat came. She updated Robert on his condition and then left. Reva stayed and chatted until lunchtime, then left for an hour.

Around two o'clock, Robert was reading the Renata file when someone knocked on his door. It was Reva. She was more somber and wearing her shoulder holster, and was accompanied with two men. He thought he recognized Caspar, but was glad when Reva confirmed their names.

"Robert, this is Caspar, and this is Michael. Caspar's been standing sentry outside. They are going to be your 24-hour in-room team until we can move you to Denver."

"What? Denver, why? I have at least three more months of physical therapy and six weeks before I can even walk again, let alone leave the hospital."

"We got an update this morning. The Renatas have declared open season on you. You're no longer safe in DC, let alone on the East Coast. Stan considered Witness Protection, but he's gonna drop you on Jonesey instead."

"Not Dave Jones, the meanest FBI agent in the west, in charge of the Denver Terrorism branch, Jonesey?"

Reva smiled, "You know him?"

Robert shook his head. "Not really, but he was in my rookie class back at the academy; and he was ruthless and driven then."

Reva sighed, "Well he's more lethal now, so you'll be fine. He's my pinch-hit partner on Stan's big cases since neither of us can stick to a permanent partner." She waved Caspar and Michael out and continued. "I'm serious, Robert, you have a full protection team here in place, 24-hours/7-days. I am going to be your last-resort, in-room, 'they go with us' protection, just in case somebody gets past Cas and Mike. They mean it." She pointed out his window. "Somebody broke in the roof access over there, and we found evidence that a sniper has scoped out your room. They want you dead."

The next three days were tense, but made better by the fact that Reva played his girlfriend in order to achieve 24-hour access to Robert's room. The staff got used to seeing her there, and began consulting with her on his care. Robert didn't mind though. Over those days, he'd discovered he really liked her, and while part of him hoped she really was single and he could get something going with her once he was better, he'd considered he'd take what hours or days he could in her company. That first night he'd watched her catnap in the recliner at the foot of his bed and admitted the truth. He had never wanted to live with another woman again after his ex-wife, but he'd give it all up if he could spend the rest of his life just staring at Reva. It had only been a couple of days, but Robert was sure he was smitten with this extremely capable, unflappable, utterly competent FBI agent. *Who probably is married to a great guy and has five kids.* He thought bitterly.

Chapter Seven
Denver and Jonesey

Robert sat in the ambulance, waiting for his escort and considering his life yet again. The Renatas' latest hit on him had changed everything. Only once that threat was gone could he return to DC. From here on, he'd be out west in Jonesey's hands.

In the weeks since the 'lavender incident' Robert gave his mother and sister power of attorney, and they'd spent days liquidating his assets under a heavy FBI guard hoping to protect them from the Renatas staking out his home. They'd sold his condo. Then, his mom and sister had moved all his stuff into storage out in Grand Junction. Once there, they'd sold his old Audi, and used the funds to procure an old Jeep Cherokee for his transportation back home in Colorado once he was better. Jonesey's crew had fitted the Cherokee for off-trail work, and his sister had loaded what she considered minimal gear for him.

Apparently, everyone figured the Renata trials could take years and that he needed to stay away from DC for the duration. Supposedly, once he got to Denver, Jonesey's crew had set up an apartment in an old-folks community where he could access 24-hour medical support and physical therapy, but be able to drive around as he liked in the jeep. Robert marveled at what the FBI could accomplish in only a couple of weeks.

He thought about his divorce and how it would affect him now. Once his ex had shown up pregnant to one of their after-divorce 'asset dispersal' meetings, a paternity test and age of the fetus shown unequivocally that she'd been unfaithful while they were still married, which rescinded the alimony. So, Robert had his funds back. His ex was also ordered to pay him half the value of the Dallas house, which gave Robert a nice nest egg. The irony was that she'd only actually agreed to divorce him after she found out she was pregnant—she'd only missed one period and figured she could hustle through divorce before anyone found out about her affair. Robert sighed. *She'd done well in her plot to get out of the marriage. No one knew she was even unhappy with me, let alone enjoying on a yearlong affair until I spotted the baby bump two months after our separation.* He smiled. *She really hated it when I dragged her back in front of the judge.*

Robert shuddered thinking about their last big fight. The divorce was nearly final and the ex had come over to see him to ensure he hadn't taken any of her stuff when he'd moved out. She'd requested a walk-through of his apartment while her boyfriend waited outside in the car. She didn't make it past the kitchen. Robert had a beef stew bubbling away on the stove, and the smell had made her nauseous. When she'd started to gag, he became suspicious and confronted her. She'd admitted to being pregnant even though they'd only been separated for eight weeks. Anger washed over Robert again. *That bitch had refused to have sex with me for SIX MONTHS prior to that point.* He'd lost his temper that day, and called his attorney as soon as the ex and her boyfriend had left his apartment. *I'm glad we had enough documentation so that the judge ordered a paternity test, which proved that the baby couldn't have been mine. Thank heavens the age of the fetus proved she'd been unfaithful before we ever separated. Damn her anyway for telling me all those years that she wasn't ready for kids when in reality she just didn't want my kids.*

Robert rolled his neck trying to loosen it. Jonesey had chartered a flight for him, and would personally escort him to the Denver safe house. Robert's mood had darkened ever since the Denver plan was announced. He supposed that he was due for a black depression, but he couldn't seem to snap out of it. He wondered whether getting to know Reva had just put a temporary hold on something inevitable. He'd lain awake throughout the night thinking about how his life that had been so newly hopeful just last week. *Stan had to put me on a medical retirement, so I have no job and only part pay from my pension. I have no home since the bitch has the Dallas house and my Mom sold my DC condo. I still need at least one surgery to repair missing muscle in my leg, and my foot bones have fused. The pain will never go away and...* Robert's thoughts stopped as a deep sadness enveloped him.

On their last day together, he and Reva had spent the day talking and laughing. She'd even taken him for a roll along the corridors with his chair. He'd refused to broach the burning questions in his heart. He wished more than ever that the torture had never happened, that his group had tasked anyone other than he and Alan for that job. *It should have killed me. Instead, here I am. Half a man, with half pay, half the friends I used to have, and no life and no chance of ever getting one again.* The tentative friendships he'd formed as a member of Stan's team would fizzle out pretty quick, once he was across the country. And, he had never really liked Jonesey, let alone got along with him.

As rookies the bigwigs thought the boys from Idaho and Colorado would bond, but he and Jonesey were oil and water. The *only* thing they had in common was having grown up LDS or Mormon. Jonesey was a good, church-attending member. Robert had been devout until he'd started a proselyting mission, but he burned out after six months and came home early in shame and disillusioned about God and life. Jonesey wasn't one to pressure him about religion, but Robert had been too touchy and snapped at Jonesey over an invitation to Sunday services. "Hell that was nearly twenty years ago. What a heck of a thing to remember about somebody." Robert said out loud.

He'd begun talking to himself in the hospital early on. When he couldn't sleep and couldn't bear to think about what he was feeling or experiencing, he needed someone to talk to, so he started talking to himself. It seemed to help, especially when he couldn't sleep, and it was the single habit, that the shrink didn't pester him to quit.

All these worries about his future or meeting Jonesey or living in Denver for the first time in sixteen years, were fruitless. He only had one real worry, and it was working itself into a huge regret as well. *Damn you. You know you could have talked to Stan about it. He'd have leveled with you and let you know whether or not you had a chance with her, but oh no, you have to freak out and go all chicken. Hell, you still don't know if she's even available.*

Robert realized he didn't care whether Reva was single or not; he was fixated on her. The further he got from her, the more convinced he was that she was the woman for him. "It's too bad it will never happen. Not with this body." Most of the folks who worked to rehabilitate him assumed Robert's issues with his body were his lack of full-function in his leg or his scars. But, neither of those things really slowed him down compared to the real problem. He'd been a healthy full-blooded male his entire life since he was twelve years old, but ever since the first morning he'd awoke in the hospital after the torture, he'd been impotent. Only he and his shrink knew and Robert wasn't ready to talk to anyone else about it. It was clearly a psychological problem, but nothing happened down there anymore. Not even night emissions. *I am truly worthless, half a man. I can't even help Stan on the old cases anymore. And there's no way I could be the man for Reva like this. You'd think meeting the woman I want for the rest of my life would have fixed it, but no. Not me. Face it Rob, you are one big loser in life.* Recriminations and sorrow made Robert hang down his head. The loop became. *I am just a useless lump of flesh. I am just useless. I am useless.* The loop kept playing in his head.

***

That's how Jonesey found him a few minutes later. Stan had briefed him on Robert's condition and he'd done a little recon on his own, after speaking to Reva. David Jones (Jonesey) looked at Robert sitting in the ambulance. It had been a hot day in DC, but the sun had gone down and a cool breeze was blowing across the tarmac. He could see the ambulance drivers over talking with some of the airport cronies out by the terminal. They'd left Robert on a wheel chair in the back of the bus, but had opened the back doors so he could see and feel the breeze.

Jonesey had seen a lot of suffering in his life and career. Robert's posture seemed to scream 'I am wounded' to him. Too many of the bad asses he hunted down in the woods had major personal problems. He remembered Robert from way back when they were twenty-something rookies and cocky out of the academy. They'd had some rough words, but had parted on 'agree to disagree' terms and had given each other a wide berth. Jonesey had stayed in DC his first year or two with the FBI, while Robert had gone out to San Francisco, because his girl was a law student at Stanford. By the time Robert had come back to DC, Jonesey was well established in the Denver office. Jonesey had wondered about that placement…There were jobs open in both offices, and he'd figured Robert, having grown up in Grand Junction, CO would jump at the Denver job, but he went to DC instead. His research had shown that posting was due to the girl too, only by then she was the wife. Robert had then moved again for his wife's career, this time to Dallas. Only the divorce a year or so ago brought him back to DC, again NOT Denver. Jonesey had planned on a fight with Robert once his sources made it clear that Robert was distanced from his family, and would go anywhere rather than Denver. *Too bad. Denver is the only place I can really keep him safe right now. He'll have to deal. I'll just work to keep his family out of his hair.*

Reva had told Jonesey a few things, mostly hinting

that Robert was a 'wounded warrior' and prone to black moods. Jonesey had noticed a note in Reva's tone that made him curious. *Once I get Robert settled I better fly to DC and get the full story out of Reevs. If I didn't know better, I'd think she was sweet on him.* Jonesey trusted his instincts in this and decided he'd move heaven and earth to help Robert heal no matter what, but especially if he was the one Reva wanted. He'd worked with Reva for a long time, and known her longer. She had yet to find someone that really suited her, and Jonesey could tell by looking at Robert that he was just her type. *If he's competent, religious, smart, and has a good sense of humor, I'll throw them together myself.* He decided. Reva deserved a good man, and from what he'd heard about Robert's ex, he too deserved a good woman.

Jonesey stopped about ten feet from the back of the ambulance and studied what he saw. Robert had clearly kept up his strength. His arms and chest were clearly defined. The right leg looked good too. He looked at the special boot on his left foot and the heavy-duty brace on the thigh, and decided the guy would be in big pain full-time. *He's looking down and that set of shoulders tells me he's not in a good place. Stan told me he was wearing the [LDS] garments, so he's gone back to church, which will help. He looks clean-shaven, but that hair is long. I think he's hurt, lost, and not sure he's going on. Mental note: No guns near him for a while.* Robert looked up at him and met his eyes. That decided him. *He'll do. He's not flinching. There's some fight left here.* He moved in, and leaned on the edge of the ambulance door.

"Leland. You look like hell. Can you walk, or are you wheeling it?"

"Same to you, Jonesey. You don't look so good for a forty-year-old skinhead wannabe. Where's your beard and fatigues? Yes, I can walk as soon as my stiches mend but not now. When I do it hurts like hell, so yes I am wheeling it for now - and the near future."

Jonesey nodded and smiled. "Whatever floats your boat. Despite our past history, a lot of water has flown under many bridges, and whatever you think of me I consider you a brother in arms and have your back. I tangled with the Renatas a time or two in my youth, and I didn't think I could keep your hide alive back east. So I am sorry to drag you to your homeland, but it's the best option we have. Besides Denver's a lot bigger maze to lose somebody in than Boise."

***

Robert considered what Jonesey said. He knew that Jonesey was a good guy and a lethal agent. Stan clearly trusted him, and even Reva figured he'd be safe with him. He considered his options. *Hell. I guess I am not ready to die, and it looks like I have just this one option to survive.* "Understood. Where's the damn plane? It better have a ramp."

Jonesey laughed and gestured over his shoulder. "That little Cessna over there. And it not only has a ramp, but a full lay-down reclining chair in the back so you can sit, stand or lay—your preference. Reva also had me stock the fridge, so right about Baltimore, you can eat your fill and sleep the rest of the way." Jonesey looked serious when he asked, "I need to know some things, off the record, so I can better help you. But they can all wait except this: Do you need any prescriptions or chemical aids?"

Robert sighed. He considered lying, just to see Jonesey's reaction. *I bet the guy's serious and would hook me up.* But, he figured Jonesey had been straight with him so he'd be straight back. "No man. I tried opiates the first few weeks, but what's wrong with me can't be fixed with oblivion. I've been living with it on just Ibuprofen or Tylenol these past 10 months. I hurt all over, but the poppy just dulls it. The pain will never go away so I figured I'd find another way to live with it."

"Thanks for leveling with me, man. We both walk a hard road, and I needed to know so I could help if needed."

"Thanks Jones. What I need is for you to lower the damn ramp so I can roll off this bus and into my next phase."

Jonesey smiled and hit the button. Jonesey and Robert walked and wheeled over the waiting plane. The pilot joined them shortly after, and Robert made it out of DC without incident.

Chapter Eight
Robert's Plane Ride to Denver

Robert tried to relax. The plane was small, but seemed comfortable. He could just see the back of Jonesey's head four rows in front of him on the first row of seats. He reclined the seat to lean his body back as the footrest elevated his legs. He had no idea how Jonesey had chartered a jet with an ergonomically proper and comfortable set of fully reclining seats in the back, but he'd not question it.

For the first time in a while, he felt truly comfortable. The seat was covered with butter-soft leather and what must be memory foam cushioning. For once, Robert could stretch out with full support under his legs that didn't inflate and deflate all the time. He sighed in satisfaction and laid his head back. The pain in his mending bones was persistent, but at least the rest of his body could be comfortable. He wasn't particularly hungry, nor tired. He didn't feel much like reading or watching a movie on the tiny seatback display in front of him. He wondered if Jonesey had a music player to lend him. He'd packed his ancient Walkman in his gear from the hospital, and wondered for the first time whether his mom and sister had packed his CDs and albums and taken them to Grand Junction or trashed them. His music collection was huge and the one thing that he'd took with him from place to place over the years. He wondered whether he should have taken up Reva's suggestion to upgrade to a smartphone, so he could have music on his phone.

Robert was trying to decide whether to get up and ask for some tunes, when Jonesey appeared next to him, startling him.

"Gee man. Sorry to startle you, but I forgot to give this to you when we took off." Jonesey held out a brand-new iPod with weird ear buds.

"What's this?"

"Well, your old team wanted to give you something to wish you well, and they contributed to this and some noise-cancelling headphones. Stan told Reva about how you hate the noisiness of planes, and she cooked this up. She also talked to your mom, and they worked together to load as much of your music as we could scrounge up amongst the music lovers in the office." Jonesey handed the player over to Robert and held up a tiny sack with spare rubber pads for the ear buds. "These Bose ear buds are something else. The silicon Spock-eared things not only pad the buds in your ears, they allow the buds to rest in your ear without putting pressure on the inner cartilage. Reva has a set and figured you'd enjoy them." Jonesey sat the paperwork and a case on the seat to Robert's left and said "Enjoy," as he turned and returned to his seat.

Robert was moved, his voice nearly broke when hollered up to Jonesey, "Thanks, man and tell them thanks too." Jonesey didn't look back, but held up is hand in acknowledgement. Robert was touched. *Bless those guys.* He messed around with the buds and decided he needed the bigger Spock-ear pads for them. He fiddled around and replaced the soft silicon pads. *Jonesey's right. These are comfortable.* He turned on the noise-cancelling function and was relieved when his world became silent. He turned it off to save the battery for now and then spotted the tiny USB charging station on the phones. There was a matching connection in the arm of his bench, so he turned the function back on and smiled as music began to play.

Robert shifted his shoulders as he started scrolling through the music library to see what his friends had loaded for him. As he scanned, tears came to his eyes as he saw the many albums and songs in the list. *I can't believe it. There's so much here. They did this all just for me?* Strong emotions choked him. His Mom must have at least catalogued his collection if she didn't move it to Grand

Junction. So many of his old LPs and CDs were here. There was also some new stuff, and his eye caught on a playlist, "Reva's songs for Robert." *She made me a playlist. I feel like I'm in high school.* Robert laughed. He barely heard Jonesey as he hollered back;

"What's so funny?"

Robert pulled out the left ear bud and replied "Nothing much. It's just that Reva made me a playlist. It's been years since a girl gave me a mix tape." Jonesey turned to look at him and cupped his hands around his mouth, "You are lucky. Reva likes you." Jonesey paused, and looked like he was considering whether or not to say something more. He continued in a more serious voice, "You better be nice to Reva. She may not have a husband, but she has a lot of lethal friends, including me." Jonesey gave a lethal smile and nodded to indicate he meant what he said, and turned back around.

Robert put his ear bud back in and considered what Jonesey had said. *So she is single. Jonesey hadn't said I couldn't go for her, only that I'd have to be good to her.* He smiled and imagined how his and Reva's next meeting could or should play out. As he daydreamed, he listened to Reva's playlist. Reva had taken a bunch of his favorite songs and chosen the best and most upbeat ones. He spent the next couple of hours picturing a long car ride in Reva's Chevelle. *That woman gets me. Somehow she really gets me. I can really groove to these.* Robert became determined. Whatever happened from here on, he was going to get better. His work friends knew him and loved him enough to give him back his music. He wasn't going to shoot his life to hell after all.

Robert considered the worst days since his torture. At first he'd tried fasting and praying for God to take his life… and one day the answer came—God told him in strong feelings and thoughts that almost became words. *Not now. Your life is not over.* God did not give him any specifics, and even if Robert had no idea what to do with his life, he'd live it. He'd started going back to physical therapy, and then he'd worked hard to recover and kept this focus even after each successive surgery.

Robert thought, *Maybe this Renata death threat was part of God's next step for me. After all, before the torture, I'd given up on God.* Robert fully admitted that it was only when he'd truly thought he would die that he'd reached out to God for the first time in years. *Now that I am finally back with Him, here I am a year later on a new path with Jonesey of all people. Jonesey is the king of hiding in the mountains. Didn't he have a great grandpa's cabin high in the wilderness of No Return…? Maybe I'll go there and get my head back together.* Robert drifted to sleep as he floated away on Reva's music and the new thoughts that made him hopeful for the future. Robert dreamed and his daydreams turned into fantasies about Reva.

***

Jonesey walked back to check on Robert as he got a cold drink from the plane's mini-fridge. Robert had the ear buds in, had tucked the iPod into his T-shirt pocket, and was sleeping. Jonesey noticed Robert's face looked content and relaxed and smiled as he went back to his seat. *He may just make it through this if I can keep him alive through the last Renata trial.*

At that moment, a dreaming Robert was skinny-dipping in the Colorado River, with Reva, in his grandpa's favorite fishing pool near the family homestead outside of Parachute, CO.

Chapter Nine
Reva's Dream

Reva's dream self was hiking a dusty and sandy trail down to a river far below. The place felt familiar, but she knew she had never been here before. Instead of the deep forests of the gently sloped Appalachian trails she was used to near DC, this trail switch-backed its way down a steep, rocky mountain. Dusty quaking aspens shaded the trail here and there, and sagebrush took up the space between clumps of rough, tall, yellow grass.

The dreaming Reva knew the trail well, and was briskly making her way down the trail. Reva felt the sun beating down on her. It was clearly a warm summer afternoon and the dust on the leaves indicated it hadn't rained recently. The trail wound down the side of a west-facing mountain that followed the riverbed. Sweat ran down her neck between her shoulder blades and she felt sweat pockets under her arms and behind her knees. Reva felt a solid walking stick in her right hand and a medium-heavy pack on her back. She knew she was in one of her favorite hiking outfits: cargo shorts, a breezy cotton button-down, a floppy hat, and her good leather hiking boots.

Reva felt a deep anticipation of the end of the trail and hurried towards it. She could hear the rushing river now. The trail had leveled out as it lost the last feet of altitude and leveled out to follow the river. The quaking aspens were thicker here, and joined by soaring cottonwoods and squat willow bushes. The grass was thick this close to the river and still green, while summer wildflowers appeared every so often. Reva saw some purple flowers with dark stripes on the petals. She heard her friend Jenny's voice calling them crows' feet. In another spot she saw a squat wild rose bush with a riot of single-petaled pink blooms. She noticed the bright green of the rose leaves and the bright yellow of the rose centers.

She hurried along and soon saw the clearing… this is why she'd been rushing down to the river. The river had a cool, deep, and secluded pool here. She wanted a cool soak and to get clean before she headed back up the mountain.

In her mind, Reva wondered what was up the mountain for a second. *What was at the top of the trail?*, but fell back into dreaming as she took off her pack and set it securely near some bushes and a big rock. She laid a towel on the bushes to warm in the sun within easy access of the rock. Then she quickly stripped down to bare skin as she carefully stowed her gear. She grabbed a small vial on a cord and slipped it around her neck and then carefully crossed the warm, sandy rocks of the riverbank to the water.

Reva luxuriated in the cool water. Ten feet away the deeper water of the main river flow rushed past her, but here she was in a small eddy pool about five feet deep where the water gently swirled around her. The riverbed here was large smooth river rocks and it was a great place for some dunking. Reva opened the vial hanging down from her neck and soaped herself with the homemade concoction. She recognized the scent of verbena. One of her holistic friends in DC made it for her. The soapy mixture was a hair/body wash and totally herbal so it wouldn't harm the environment. Reva used it when she was out on the trail. Reva leaned her head back in the water to let the gentle current soak the suds out of her curls. Her friend also made an oil-based rub for her hair after it was washed to help condition the curls, which had a tendency to dry out. In the dream, Reva thought of the herbal oil and resolved to treat her hair once she was done playing in the water. Dreaming Reva had no worries about anyone spotting her. When awake Reva asked why, dreaming Reva just thought, *It's private property, no one else has access to the trail or this spot and the river's main current is too rough for fishing over there.*

She floated and splashed for a long time. Reva loved the green color of the river water. It clearly wasn't emerald, but a deep grassy green like pine needles. *Weren't rivers supposed to be blue or brown?* That thought didn't bother dreaming Reva. She was enjoying the sparkling sun on the water, the feeling of being clean again, and the dappled sunshine through the leaves above the pool.

Reva was standing on a large rock at the bottom of the pool and leaning her head back to give her hair a last soak. She held up her right hand and noticed that her fingers were wrinkled from the water. *Time to get out.* She sighed, and dunked down for a final rinse. Reva popped up out of the water and used both hands to move her dripping hair back from her face. She swiped the water from her eyes and brows and blinked a few times to get her bearings and started. There was a man standing in the water in front of her a few feet away looking at her.

In the dream, Reva smiled at him, but in her conscious mind she worried about him—who is he? He appeared to be naked, he was clearly bare-chested. But, in the dream Reva was thinking "What a chest!" in 'yummy' tones. The man was well-built and tanned with dark hair and a slight beard and mustache, and he was coming closer. Soon Reva felt him reach her and envelop her in his arms. As the dream Reva stretched up to meet his kiss, their chests touched, and awake Reva finally recognized the man and her shock woke her up. *Oh my God. It's Robert, he's healed and he looks so happy. We fit together so well.*

Reva sat up on her comfortable first-class seat. She was fully awake now, but the dream was still strong in her head coloring her life. *I've never been on that trail, but I knew it.* Reva tried hard to clear her thoughts. She looked at her watch, *Five hours to DC—SIGH.* She tried to breathe deeply to clear her head. She felt overheated.

Reva caught the stewardess's eye and she returned with a cool drink. Reality descended on Reva. *I've had that same dream before, I didn't remember it as clearly as just now, but that's the dream I had the morning I flew to Tel Aviv. I must be fixated on Robert.* Reva closed her eyes and tried to focus on the cold Sprite bubbles in her mouth. Her brother had flown her to Tel Aviv to see Grandma on her birthday, round-trip/first-class no less. Reva looked down at herself in an effort force her mind back to reality. *Here you are on a plane home to the states.* She felt the smooth silk of her shirt and the heavy pearls around her neck. She'd bound her curls into an elegant chignon and wore smooth slacks that matched her taupe slippers perfectly. *I'm the classic image of a Jewish princess going home to her New York penthouse. That dusty skinny-dipper is just a fantasy I made up.* Reva resolved to forget about Robert, who was right now somewhere in Colorado with Jonesey trying to learn to walk again. *Rein it in. The Renatas are still after him, and it will be a year before he's fully healed. You probably won't see him again, so move on. You have got to stop these thoughts.* On that advice, Reva stowed her drink, turned towards the window on her right, and fell back into sleep—dreamless this time.

Chapter Ten
Robert in Wilderness of No Return

Robert hated nights like this. Before the divorce he and his wife had alternated celebrating Friday nights by either working late and falling into bed exhausted or arguing about money or kids. To Robert fifteen years had seemed like plenty of time for his wife to 'live her life' and 'build a career', but she always insisted that she wasn't ready for children.

He should have known better. Amanda's expensive tastes and obsessions about her personal appearance should have been warning signs to him—that they'd never mesh. When she'd finally been able to buy the brand-new Lexus she'd always wanted, he'd thought that would satisfy her, or at least allow her enough personal satisfaction that she would relax and enjoy being with him. But, no, Amanda had grown into a vain and selfish person. Robert had heard people talk about 'growing apart,' but he'd never believed it, until it happened to his own marriage.

While he'd studied criminal justice and police science in school, Amanda had been immersed in her business management classes. When she'd been accepted into the law program at Stanford, she'd finally married him. He'd shared her excitement about her career and even helped support her until she'd finished law school. When he'd chosen to work for the FBI, he was grateful that his federal service would help pay off his student loans and moved to the San Francisco office for her. Amanda hadn't really noticed. When she landed a beginning career position with a huge law firm in DC who paid her massive student loans off immediately, she'd considered it her due to have someone pay the loans off for her. She never mentioned them again. She'd also made him move to DC for the firm. Then she'd made him move once again to Dallas, again for the firm. When he'd noticed her shame about being so 'poor' while they were living off the relatively small FBI salary Robert should have known. He should have known to worry about his wife and their marriage.

Robert felt old today and a failure. He turned forty years old the week before and had little to show for his life so far. He knew that Stan sent him out west in an attempt to keep him a viable agent in addition to protecting him from the Renatas. That morning when Jonesey had picked him up in Denver, Robert realized that Stan was *really* worried about him. He wondered, *Does Stan think I need some heavy baby-sitting? If so, I'm in trouble. Maybe this is for the best.* He could no longer live the way he'd had, but he wanted to.

For now he'd let Jonesey take care of him and thankfully, Jonesey wasn't one to judge. But, Robert was. He knew that what he'd experienced months ago after his wounds had gone septic and nearly died was clinically classified as a 'breakdown.' Stan had even admitted the doctors considered he'd had a psychic break when Robert had pressed the issue. But, Jonesey didn't care. He'd settled Robert in his own cabin in a heart-wrenchingly beautiful Alpine valley perfect for a peaceful and private recovery.

Jonesey had delivered a month's worth of groceries quietly with a parting statement, "Hey man, we all need some space and time to ourselves. Call me when you are ready to come back down off the mountain."

Robert thought about where he would work in the FBI if he survived this Renata thing. He'd left Dallas after the divorce and transferred back to DC, hoping that the busy DC FBI office would help him recover from his divorce. Instead he'd spent a lot of time going through the motions up to the grocery torture. He was sure that Stan knew about his poor performance now. *Grant probably gave him an earful besides all those notes in my personnel file. I'll probably be the same whether I go back to DC or stay in Boise or Denver. My work problems are my problems, not my supervisor's.* Robert sighed. He couldn't worry about the job right now. Besides, he wasn't as sure as Stan was that he could go back to his old FBI job. Without his partner, he was just an *almost-lethal* shell of his old self.

Robert thought of Reva and his impotence and wondered whether he'd ever have a sex-life again. His divorce had been final for nearly three years now. Amanda had married that senior partner in her firm once she'd given him a fine son and heir. *It doesn't even matter anymore that Amanda wouldn't have my son. If Reva came here today and asked to have my babies, I couldn't no matter how bad I want to.*

Chapter Eleven
DC Renata Trial

Reva rushed up the stone steps in the federal courthouse. She needed to get a message to Stan now. She held up her badge to the bailiff guarding the closed courtroom door. He pointed to the clock behind her showing it was two minutes to the hour, "Not now, the Judge is advising the jury. They'll break in two minutes." Reva stood and tried not to tap her foot in impatience. However, unlike other federal judges she'd known over the years, Judge Burnham was punctual. At the top of the hour, the bailiff inside cracked the door to speak to the outside guards. The bailiff Reva could see nodded to her and opened the door allowing her in before he opened both doors to allow the Renata trial spectators and officers out.

Reva found Stan sitting with Grant a couple of rows behind the prosecution bench talking to one of the Attorney General's top investigators. The men looked up when she approached,

Reva handed Stan a piece of paper. "I'm calling Jonesey. We caught a Renata in Denver."

Stan read the message Reva had written and then passed it on to Grant who read it also and then handed it to the investigator.

Stan said, "Give that to your boss. Our Denver team has phone surveillance where we caught Luke Renata authorizing the Denver hit on Robert. His brother Clyde was also on the line. Have your boss call us tomorrow."

The investigator nodded, and then asked, "What about Leland? We may need him to testify to corroborate."

Stan looked to Grant who nodded, and his response to the Department of Justice (DOJ) investigator was emphatic, "Not now. The Renata hit man traced Robert to our safe house's neighborhood in Denver. He didn't get to the house or spot any of our team, but he got *within a mile of Robert in Denver.* Your office assured us that as far as the Renatas were concerned, Robert was in a secure wing of Walter Reed." Stan pointed a finger at the investigator, his temper rising, "No. You can't have Robert. We're taking no chances bringing him back here. Luke shouldn't even have had access to a phone; you people are slipping."

Stan turned back to shake Grant's hand and then left the courthouse with Reva.

Reva spoke first, "I am so glad Robert moved six weeks ago."

Stan nodded, "When you get back to the office to call Jonesey, conference in Mitch in Salt Lake. I don't know where they have Robert since they moved him from Denver, but they need to be prepared for more Renatas. I'll work with DOJ to see if we can cut off the remaining family funds. Meanwhile see if Mitch and Jonesey can think of another spot to stash Robert. I don't want to lose another agent to the Renatas!"

Reva nodded, leaving Stan in his office as she went to her desk. Thoughtfully she tapped the phone against her lower lip as she thought about Mitch and Jenny Harper. Mitch was an old FBI colleague of her and Jonesey. He'd left Stan's terrorist team and the DC FBI office back in 2002 for Salt Lake City, Utah. Reva sighed. She always felt wistful when she thought about how happy Mitch and Jenny were. She and Jenny were still friends this many years later.

The FBI had used Jenny on a terrorist capture back in 2001 and she and Mitch had really hit it off. However, after the successful mission, something had fractured their new romance, and caused Jenny to leave DC for her native Utah. Everyone had figured Mitch would get over it, until he'd gone out with the FBI force helping with security during the Winter Olympics held in Salt Lake City, Utah in early 2002. Mitch had gone out there looking for Jenny who'd lived north of Salt Lake. They'd gotten past whatever issue had broke them up during that visit and Mitch had never returned to DC.

Reva sighed. Mitch had been more lethal than Jonesey and a great agent for Stan. However, once he'd married Jenny, Mitch was content to be a domesticated FBI operative inside the relatively small Salt Lake office. He spent his days doing baby-FBI work all over Utah when he wasn't helping Jonesey on big assignments. *I bet if Jonesey's run out of spots to hide Robert in Denver or Boise, he'll take him down to Mitch and tuck Robert in somewhere deep with the Mormons.* Reva smiled, she knew that Jenny was proud of domesticating Mitch and would love to pamper Robert.

Reva felt a deja-vu moment. She'd had that river dream with Robert again this morning, but this time she'd remembered why; it was Jenny's voice naming the wildflowers. Jenny was an expert on Intermountain flora, and if her voice named the flower, Reva knew the recurring dream happened somewhere out west. To have Stan mention Mitch today, after Reva had dreamed about Jenny this morning seemed like a sign. Reva consciously squashed those thoughts. *There's no way I am going to end up in Colorado naked with Robert in a river. I am NOT.*

She worked to picture Jenny in her kitchen then saw her molly-coddling Robert there. With her focus reestablished, Reva dialed the phone, "Hey Jonesey, it's Reva. Stan has a message and wants to pull Mitch in our bear hunt. Yeah. The hunters are getting close and Stan thinks Mitch can find a cave for the bear to hibernate over the winter."

Chapter Twelve
Robert in Wilderness of No Return—Still

Robert stood on the hundred-and-fifty-year-old wooden planks that supported the porch on Jonesey's family cabin, trying to keep his balance as the large punch bag came at his still-weak left side. As he focused on balance and strength exercises along his left side, Robert continued to pummel the bag with both hands and let his thoughts run free. Over the past six weeks his mood and condition had greatly improved.

He considered his family. He'd been in the West for six months but had only spoke to his dad so far. Robert smiled when he thought of that. *Bless Jonesey for his connections.* Jonesey had a car dealer buddy in Grand Junction and he'd used his buddy to help smuggle Robert's dad to him into Denver, when the buddy brought up his outfitted Jeep. It was a perfect cover. Robert's dad drove the souped-up Jeep to Denver from Grand Junction, where the Leland family had packed it full of gear for Robert. In return, Robert's dad would then take a new car back to the dealership. This would keep him off the Renata radar. Stan had confirmed the Renatas had goons in Grand Junction and around Denver watching Robert's family for a sign of Robert.

Robert felt happiness when he thought of his dad, unlike his mom. His family problems had everything to do with his mother, but it was hard to avoid one without avoiding both. Robert's dad was well aware that Robert couldn't stand how his mom and sister treated him. His mother had never approved of Amanda and when Robert left Denver to follow Amanda to Stanford, she'd lost her temper and had been angry over 'the hold that no-good woman has over you' ever since. She'd added her resentment of his choice in wife to her disappointment in him for leaving his LDS mission years before.

Robert thought about all the reasons that his mom railed at him. He could list them and decided to, just for fun.

1. We lived together before we were married. Mom can never forgive me for sleeping with someone before marriage. She hated that it got me sent home from my mission and kicked out of the church.

2. Amanda never wanted to have kids, and I let her sway me, which denied Mom her grandbabies.

Robert shook his head and hit the bag harder. "Like I could do anything about that. Damn woman would have probably aborted, had she gotten pregnant."

3. I went to DC instead of coming home to Colorado when I left Amanda and the asshole in Dallas.

"Yeah, like I want to be mother-henned in my hometown while the Leland women parade all the eligible Mormon girls in my face."

Finally, Number 4, at least this is the last thing. I think she's angry with me because I let those bad guys nearly kill me.

This one was the easiest and hardest to refute. He sighed and paused for a minute to catch his breath. "Mom never liked me going into the FBI, and she's always expected the job to kill me. Maybe it was my fault. Did I take too many chances? Did my actions put the Renatas onto me and Alan somehow?"

Robert went back to punching the heavy bag, and pushed against the bag every few hits to build up his left side. He tried to ram the bag as hard as he could then he tried to weather the rebound. He considered what he'd done right in his life. *I followed the woman I loved and supported her career and, as much as possible, her decisions. When that failed I went back to God, fixed my life and rejoined the church. Heck I'm even living as a better Mormon than I did on my mission. Hopefully I can return to Grand Junction, but only on my terms. Mom'll have to accept that.*

Robert felt a deep gratitude for his healing body. In the past two years, he had regained a lot of the function in his leg, and was building back his endurance. He thought of his dad. *Jonesey surprised me there, by taking me to pick up the Jeep one night without warning.* Jonesey had said, "Let's get a bite to eat. You need a break from institutional food."

He'd driven Robert from the care center to an industrial section of Denver. Just as Robert recognized the lot as the main dealers' auction area he'd spotted a black, classic Jeep Cherokee with meaty tires and a gear rack on the roof - and his dad standing next to it. Robert hadn't seen his dad in nearly a year, and was grateful that he could stand upright long enough to hug him.

It was good to see his father in person. The similarities between them were still there. Of a similar height, both men's hair had a little more gray. Robert's lay more around his temples, but his Dad's had faded to a salt and pepper gunmetal-gray all over.

"I love you, son. I worried that I'd never see you standing again. Praise God that you made it through."

"Love you too, Dad. I've missed you."

They'd stood and visited for nearly a half-hour, before Jonesey's buddy came with the dealer transfer car and they'd all left the lot.

Robert's dad had suggested a boxing routine to help build his balance and endurance. He'd found an old set of boxing gloves, a speed bag, and a heavy bag and put them in the Jeep with Robert's FBI tactical gear. The physical therapist agreed and worked with the residency staff to outfit Robert's patio with the boxing bags. They put a second speed bag at a lower level so Robert could work out with it from his chair when he couldn't stand. Beating things with his fists was a great pressure release for Robert and he took to the physical therapist's boxing routine.

Jonesey noticed the improvement in Robert's physicality soon after, so that when Robert was ready to leave the care center Jonesey agreed to set up the boxing bags at his old family cabin. He even let Robert help him heft the heavy bag up to the porch. Robert kept a prayer of gratitude in his heart at all times—for the many good things that had happened in his life after the awful injuries he'd suffered. Every step he took, each hike he completed and each pounding from the heavy bag he survived, seemed like a mini-miracle to him.

After an hour or so, Robert hiked down the cabin's path to the nearby Frank Church - River of No Return for his daily dunking. He'd spent all summer here in the cabin, and Jonesey came every couple of weeks with some fresh laundry and other supplies. Jonesey had spent the first week helping him find his way around, but mostly chopping wood for the cabin. Since then Robert had worked on his strength, so that he now could chop wood for an hour at a time. He also improved his mobility and could now easily manage the quarter-mile trek to the river. Jonesey had given him a tiny pedometer so he could measure his progress and he'd even completed the 7-mile hike to the nearest road, which led to the tiny airstrip maintained by the forestry officers who patrolled the wilderness area. The rangers would often stop by to have breakfast with Robert, when their patrol neared Jonesey's cabin. All the rangers got to know the few families who had land or cabins grandfathered in the wilderness area. They liked getting to know the few 'locals' and many of them knew Jonesey and his family well. In fact, they depended on Jonesey's intense knowledge of this area of the wilderness area, and usually used him when conducting a search and rescue mission.

Robert had developed a routine that worked for him. He'd get up and box for an hour or two before breakfast. Then he'd cook up something brunch-like and big and then hike down to the river for the day's water.

While it boiled for cleaning on the cabin's cast-iron woodstove he'd chop a load of wood, and then wash up. He'd spend the remainder of each day hiking around the wilderness, walking down to say 'hi' to the rangers at the airstrip or just wander along the river watching the wildlife. He'd have a snack lunch while he was out.

Robert always returned to the cabin in late afternoon. He'd putter around the cabin while he cooked his dinner, then he'd read or listen to music until he was tired. Often he'd wind the hand-cranked USB charger for his iPod, as he sat on Jonesey's grandpa's rocking chair on the porch watching the sunset. Some nights he would listen to the news on the AM/FM emergency radio. Jonesey kept him in batteries and had also installed a solar-powered mini-radio tower, so he could radio out for help if needed. The rangers would sometimes contact Robert via this with messages for him they'd received via relay to the airstrip.

Robert relished the chores he'd do to while away the hours. He'd learned to mend his clothing while on his mission and enjoyed repairing them here. He was surprised at the hard wear they could take. It seemed he was mending some torn bits each week. He'd also started whittling to kill time, and that morphed into carving. There was wood around, and Robert began enjoying making wooden bowls for the fun of seeing a block turn into something so smooth. Jonesey encouraged Robert in everything he did, and had made no comment about Robert's thoughts about carving during one trip. But had returned the next week with a full carving kit and sandpaper.

Robert smiled whenever he thought of his bowls. The wood told him what size bowl it wanted to be, and each was unique. Jonesey had handed each completed bowl over to Amy, who sold them in a small art gallery in Boise. They were becoming collectible and making some 'mad money', which he'd try to give to Robert, but Robert refused it. He insisted the Joneses keep all the proceeds in repayment for their help. Robert worked hard to ensure he made enough money to compensate Jonesey for all the supplies and gear he'd shared.

Months ago, and a lifetime away, Robert recalled his shrink telling him to go somewhere peaceful and just heal. He could hear him saying, "Give yourself time. Your mind and body need to recover and you need to allow yourself to heal." Robert had tried to do this in each place he'd found himself, but this quiet cabin in the middle of nowhere was the first spot where he actually felt the healing happen.

Robert tipped the large bowl, his last, upright on his lap. He felt along the outside with his fingers and hands in a last check of the polishing. He repeated the process as he felt along the lip and inside of the bowl. "All done. This should hold Amy's full batch of rolls," he remarked thinking of Amy's Sunday dinners. "Time to call Jonesey and go home."

It had been a good summer, but the nights were getting colder. Robert quashed the anxiety in his chest when he thought about going back to civilization.

"It's time. You know it is. It's been two years since the grocery store, and you are healthier than anybody expected. You can even go without the chair for weeks on end. It's time to go back. And, even if you never get to Grand Junction, it's better that you stay in Denver until the last Renata trial, and then you can go home." *Wherever that is,* Robert thought.

***

"Hey Jonesey, it's Mitch. Did Reva call you with the latest news?" Mitch stared out the window of his house watching his wife, Jenny tussle on the grass with two of their kids as he listened to Jonesey's response. "Yeah, if Denver's too hot, bring him here. Me and Jenny can keep Robert safe and off the Renata radar until spring."

Jenny looked up at him and waved.

Mitch waved back and ended the call with, "Ok. We'll be here. I'll get the basement ready. Safe travels." He hung up his phone and went outside to make sure his wife and four kids could handle a wounded warrior camping out with them for the winter.

Chapter Thirteen
Meet the Harpers

"Knock, Knock. Hey Harpers, anyone home?" Jonesey let himself into the house through the back porch door into the kitchen. "Hey Jenny. Is Mitch around? Do you have room for a couple extra mouths at your table this fine Sunday afternoon?"

"Sure Jonesey, any time for you. Did you bring Amy and the kids with you this time?" Jenny responded.

"No. No. Just me and a buddy. I'll introduce you when he gets here... In the meantime, where's that husband of yours?" Jonesey asked looking around the kitchen counter into the dining room beyond.

Jenny smiled at his distraction. She could always tell when Jonesey was on assignment. He always checked in with Mitch and the office before heading out to Heaven-knows-where, especially when reporting to the Salt Lake City FBI office. He was late once, and his supervisor called Mitch, because the whole office knew Jonesey won't set foot in the Salt Lake office until he's seen Mitch first. *I'll bet he's finally brought down that guy Mitch's supposed to hide.* She chuckled and pointed past Jonesey to the door he entered through. "Mitch and Danny are out in the shed. The truck lost its serpentine belt at church. They are taking inventory to see what they need to get tomorrow to fix it."

Jonesey shook his head, "You two, still driving that old clunker. You should get a new one like me." He turned on his heel and headed out stating, "Ok, then, let me check in and I'll be back in ASAP."

Jonesey found Mitch and his oldest son, Danny on a stool with Jenny's old truck's hood up. "Hey Mitch, hey Danny. Mitch, you got a minute?" Jonesey asked as he approached.

A few minutes later Jenny watched from the kitchen window as Mitch and Jonesey headed out front. She moved to the front room and saw Jonesey's brand-new, black Cadillac parked behind an older black Jeep. A tall, brown-haired guy with a cane and a limp greeted Mitch and shook his hand. The group came towards the front door and Jenny rushed to open it. Jenny spoke before either Jonesey or Mitch could, "Hey, you must be Robert. Mitch told me about you. Make yourself at home." Jenny grabbed her purse and car keys and kissed Mitch on the cheek, "Hey Honey, gotta run to Mom's. I'll be back later. Love ya." Jenny rushed out the house and purposely herded the kids into the van. *I'll take the kids to Mom's so the boys can get Robert settled in.*

***

"Thanks, Mitch, for letting me crash here for a few weeks." Robert hefted his heavy duffel in one hand as he followed him into his and Jenny's house.

"No problem, man. As you can see, we have the room with four full bedrooms upstairs, and another down, plus the open rec' room down here." Mitch carried Robert's bedroll and laundry bag into the side door and down two flights of stairs into his basement. What had been a coal storage area in the 1890s was now a spacious TV room behind a new gas furnace. Mitch and Jenny had put up a few walls to make a separate bedroom and bathroom in the other half of the basement, but kept the rest open for things like kids' sleepovers.

Robert smiled as he watched Mitch drop his bedroll on a massive camping cot and then walk the laundry over ten feet to the washer and dryer.

He looked around and then to Mitch who apologized, "Sorry for a lack in privacy, you don't have a door on your room."

"Hey, it looks good. Don't forget I've spent the last three months in an 1850s, one-room log cabin with no plumbing."

The two men laughed.

"You'll have the run of the place during the day while the kids are in school and I'm at work. Jenny will be in the sunroom working from home until two each day, but then I figure you can both work out a routine. You're welcome to share meals with us and take part in any family stuff you'd like. You can also ignore the heck out of us and do your own thing."

"Thanks, Mitch. I'll need to get my bearings and then I'll let you know."

Once Mitch left, Robert began unpacking. A few minutes later he heard him call Stan with a status report. Sure that he didn't want to hear that conversation, Robert put in his ear buds and spent the rest of the afternoon stowing his gear in the back shed. He'd decide what he'd need for a kitchen system once Jenny got home. Jonesey had told him about Jenny and Mitch Harper and swore they were glad to take him in for the winter. Robert knew that Stan would like him to return to DC once the Renata threat was neutralized, but no one in his FBI family wanted to rush him home to Grand Junction, either.

Jonesey had ferried Robert down to Ogden, Utah explaining that he wanted him to visit with the Harpers while he continued to Denver. Then, mid-trip Jonesey had alerted him to the current Renata threat and explained they wanted him to stay with Mitch for a while. Robert knew that Jonesey often would drop in on Mitch in Ogden on his way to Denver or Phoenix from Boise. Robert remembered Mitch from his early days at the FBI, but had never got to work with him personally. He'd asked Jonesey how the most-lethal and best terrorist guy in DC had ended up in BFE Utah.

Jonesey had just smiled and said, "It'll make sense when you meet Jenny."

That fired Robert's imagination. He'd known about Jonesey's Amy back in the day, but she was a normal FBI wife, and Robert imagined agents gossiped about Jonesey and Amy the way they'd done about himself and Amanda when they were still together. Robert couldn't fight his curiosity about Mitch and Jenny, but there was nobody left in DC to ask about Mitch except Reva, and he wasn't sure he wanted to talk to her just yet. None of his new buddies had known Mitch and his old partner Bill in their heyday. Robert had asked Stan about Mitch, and even he had said,

"You'll see. It all changed, once Mitch met Jenny. But, that's a story not mine to tell." Used to the normal old-lady gossips in his Dallas FBI group, Robert was shocked that everyone in DC was so closed-mouthed. Jenny and Mitch must have either a really pitiful or one unbelievable love story for everyone to be so quiet about it.

Wandering around their house, Robert could see that Jenny and Mitch were deliriously happy and living the American dream in Ogden. Their house was spacious, comfortable, and filled with beautiful pictures and homey touches. He knew the Ogden office was a tiny satellite to the FBI's Salt Lake City office, and that all the intermountain FBI agents worked together on big assignments, but he wondered what Mitch spent his days doing. Those thoughts made Robert think about what he would do once he was 'fully recovered.' *It's not like I could go undercover with the mobsters again.* He realized. He decided to pin Mitch down one day to find out what it was like to live small in the FBI after you'd lived big.

Robert was loading his second batch of clothes into Jenny's washer having got the first batch into the dryer, when he heard the back door open. For a second, his instincts took over and he panicked and backed into the corner behind the basement's support beam beside the furnace. He heard a female voice calling,

"Robert? Hey Robert, are you down there?"

Then Jenny, a tall woman with long golden-blond hair swinging in a braid came down the last stairs. Seeing her again, Robert knew why Mitch had left DC. Grateful he'd been scared for no reason, he moved out from the corner, as if he'd just turned away from the washer, "Hey, Jenny. We weren't formally introduced." He held out his hand, "Mitch said I could make myself at home, so I have commandeered your washer and dryer."

Jenny shook his hand and stared at him with an appraising look, "Hi, Robert. When Mitch and Jonesey said you'd be coming down to stay with us, I wasn't sure what to expect, but Reva's right. You are one, tall, handsome man." Jenny shocked him.

Robert quickly recovered, "You know Reva?"

"Oh sure, she was part of Mitch's team when I worked with Stan's group back in 2001."

Robert then couldn't hold back his second question, "Reva said that about me? Wow. Last time I saw her, I was looking peaked and stuck in a hospital bed." Robert's mind was reeling as Jenny continued.

"Well you know, Reva. She's a keen observer and I bet even if you were covered with pink and purple spots or wrapped in bandages she noticed your fine physique, mister. Anyway, I don't mean to embarrass you. I'll leave you down here while I get started on dinner. You have an hour until the horde descends. I'll be upstairs if you need me." With that Jenny turned and went back upstairs; clearly not worried that Robert may have a response.

Robert watched her go and then turned back to his laundry. *Figures that Jenny knows Reva, I'd better tread carefully. Wait; maybe I can use their friendship to my advantage…*

Robert stood for a moment and considered Jenny. Clearly she was beautiful and perfect for Mitch in height and looks. She was also fast. From watching her and hearing her talk, he'd peg Jenny as a Mach 1 speedster. He'd bet she was a fast driver as well as a fast talker. He'd noted intelligence in her too. She knew exactly what she was saying, and if the females in his own family were

75

anything to go by, he'd bet she'd dropped Reva's name purposely. Robert's eyes narrowed as he considered that possibility. *Reva's one of the few agents I've met that worked with both Mitch and Bill, and if she was part of the Gooding group in the summer of 2001, then she definitely got to know Jenny. No wonder that the two of them are buddies. I know Amy knows Reva and they talk now and then, but I didn't expect Reva to know Mitch and Jenny too. I better be careful.* Then his thoughts were hijacked with speculation at Jenny's statement. *Does Reva think I am sexy? God, I hope so.* He smiled wide. *I might not be at one hundred percent yet, but thoughts like that are enough to make me bounce through today.* Robert wasn't even ashamed to admit it.

Reva would trip through his thoughts now and then, and truthfully, she was the number one reason Robert would return to the DC FBI office. *What I wouldn't do for just once chance to be her man.* Robert thought. His shrink had told him to plan long-term as well as short-term goals as part of his recovery, and Robert had fixated on one-long term hope that he couldn't quite call a goal yet. He wanted more than anything to be healed and whole, and a whole man for Reva. He prayed for just one chance to be a real man in her eyes. *If I get a shot at her, I am going to take it.*

Chapter Fourteen
Hibernating in Utah

Robert found he fit in well with Jenny and Mitch and their family. Jenny and Mitch had four kids, three boys, and one girl: Daniel (Danny)-11, Lisette-10, Henry-9, and Conner-8. Daniel was an independent sort, Lisette always had her head in a book, but otherwise followed her mom around, and Henry and Conner were inseparable troublemakers. Robert got along well with everyone and made friends with each of the kids. Mitch and Jenny also ran an iron-disciplined household. Things could get rowdy, but respect was word one with the kids, and they were amazingly behaved especially when Mitch or Jenny reined in their herd.

Everyone in the Harper house had chores around the house, and they were delighted when Robert asked to be included. He relished a happy home life, and loved doing dishes. The Harpers soon sucked him into their routines in a mutually beneficial arrangement.

Robert also appreciated how Mitch let him monopolize a lot of Jenny's time. When she wasn't wife-ing her husband or mothering her kids, she was nurturing Robert. He'd decided the woman was either a first-class empath or that that she really understood him. No one else understood Robert so well. Once he got over the eeriness of having Jenny know what he wanted before he could voice the want, Robert gave in and just went with the Harper flow.

Jenny did more than anyone else to help Robert regain his sociality. She let him putter in her house, took him with her when she was doing her errands, and introduced him to her large family. Her Johnson clan was varied and helpful, and only too happy to support Jenny and Mitch's friend. Robert learned to live the 'Mi casa—Su Casa' lifestyle, and he found he loved it.

Things went well until mid-November. The one place Robert would not go was a grocery store. Everyone sympathized and no one pushed him to go grocery shopping. Jenny even made it a fun game to plan his menus using different items. She would then go get the groceries and work with Robert to try out new recipes. She'd really helped him expand his palette.

Then one November Saturday, Robert felt like he was using Jenny as a crutch when it came to his groceries. He woke up thinking that he should try it on his own, or he would never be able to live independently. He squashed any thoughts about grocery delivery and resolved to ask Jenny to take him with her today. Jenny was skeptical, but willing. He asked Jenny to only take him to grocery stores that had the produce on the right; the Renata's store in DC had the produce on the left and near the front, and to keep him away from the meat counter. Jenny also asked him about color schemes and other questions trying to get a feel for the Renata grocery. She decided the biggest grocer in town would fit the bill, and took Robert with her. Jenny took care to walk by him, but let him push the cart so he could have some control. Robert felt fine as they entered the store. It was a newer store with wood-like tiles and a snazzy black and red color scheme. Robert did fine. They had the cart nearly full, when a produce worker came by with a cart of old produce he was taking to the back of the store.

Later Robert explained it was the smell of rotten tomatoes that did it. One minute he was picking an instant oatmeal flavor with Jenny, and the next he was laying on his back staring at the grocery ceiling. Jenny said that he'd passed out and collapsed. By the time he'd come to, Mitch, who'd been working at the Ogden FBI office a few blocks over, was there with the Grocery Manager. Mitch helped him up, and then Robert started hyperventilating. It was better out in the parking lot, but he was still hyperventilating when the EMTs came a couple of minutes later. The EMT gave him oxygen and helped him concentrate on his breathing. Meanwhile, Jenny and Mitch explained Robert's situation. That day left Robert with a nasty goose egg on his head, a $100 store card and the knowledge that even when making progress, he could have a really bad day.

That night, he'd been too upset to eat dinner, and had retreated into the basement. He'd assured Jenny he'd be fine, but had a heart-to-heart talk with Mitch later that night. Robert had been grateful for what he had to say and went to sleep thinking about Mitch's explanation as to why he'd left DC,

"Hey man, I had to leave. I watched some guy try to kill my woman more than once. At the end of that summer, even though I'd thought I'd lost her, my heart wasn't in it anymore. When I found her, I knew that I never wanted to risk her again, and my career was nothing if I couldn't have her. So I followed her out here to Utah and here I stay, doing small things for the FBI. Meanwhile the biggest thing in my life, my family, stays safe and my kids can grow up happy and untouched by the ugly things in this world. Ask Jonesey what I used to be like. You are not alone in this. There are just some things that I can no longer do, and I've had to live with that knowledge. Even now, after more than ten years, I have small regrets but reap greater benefits."

Robert waited until the next day to call Jonesey, and that helped too.

Jonesey gave him some advice about living with demons, and then had closed the conversation with, "You don't see me living in DC anymore. I couldn't do it either."

Robert didn't know whether to be heartened or dismayed that these two killer FBI guys had things in their lives they avoided. So, he called his shrink, who managed to convince him to put off grocery stores for a while.

Both Jenny and Robert seemed to recover after the

'buying groceries' incident. Both agreed it was a setback, and they worked to find other ways for Robert to find self-sufficiency.

Jenny remained worried about Robert and around Christmas, when she noticed that he started closing in on himself, inspiration struck her and she called Jonesey for advice. Maybe they could find a service animal for Robert. Jenny and Jonesey had a mutual friend who raised German Shepherds for law enforcement. This trainer also worked with dogs that didn't quite meet the law-enforcement standards and helped them become service dogs for ex-military and ex-law enforcement personnel dealing with PTSD and other disorders. Jonesey said he'd call the trainer and find out what options could work for Robert. His timing was perfect. The trainer had had one dog returned to her from a local Utah K-9 unit, after the dog and his officer were in a traffic accident. The dog had survived, but the police officer had not, and the dog was inconsolable and needed a new human.

Jonesey called Jenny and one day later, the trainer dropped by Jenny's house with a golden-colored German shepherd dog, Sam to meet Robert.

Robert and Sam hit it off immediately and became inseparable. The trainer trained Robert how to take care of Sam and Jenny and Mitch supported him. The Harpers enjoyed having a dog in the house, and Sam helped Robert regain some of his independence.

In January, Robert tried a grocery store expedition one more time and successfully used his $100 card. Sam made it possible. He proudly wore his service-dog placard and helped Robert focus on something good in the worst possible places. By February no one could tell that Robert had ever had a problem going shopping. He and Jenny expanded their recipe experiments to include homemade, designer dog food for Sam.

Chapter Fifteen
Reva, I Have a Job for You

Reva dropped her latest Renata case file off at her desk. Over the past year, she'd been Grant's liaison with Stan over the mob trials against the Renatas. Stan asked that Grant update his team on the trials so he could know when it would be safe to bring back Robert.

Reva considered the stack of paperwork on her desk and thought about her career lately. *Stan has clearly been grooming me to take over his job*, she mused. *Too bad I am not interested, or maybe not yet.* Even with all her experience and years of service, she just wasn't ready to be a boss. Lately, Stan had turned over the team's old case files to her, as he continued to use her as a second in command. This allowed her to keep her training schedule in the gym.

Reva looked over at her desk phone. The indicator was red, showing she had a voicemail. Absently she dialed her inbox and waited for the message. Jonesey's voice shocked her.

"Hey Reevs. Happy birthday yesterday and happy nineteenth year with the FBI! Of course I only remembered because you are two years behind me and I got my official twenty-one-year notice today. But anyway, talk with Stan. I want you out here for a minute. Got a job for you. Could take six weeks, not sure. I asked Stan to reassign you to me for a time. Let me know what he says and whether you're up for it. Bye."

Reva looked around the office. Things were very quiet today. With Presidents Day on Monday, most of the staff had taken today off or were on assignment. *Looks like it's just him and me today. I love the Friday before a holiday.* She poked her head into Stan's office, "Hey Stan, you busy?"

"Not at all, I was hoping you'd drop by before

81

heading out today. Did Jonesey call you?"

Her eyes narrowed, "You know about that, huh. Yes, I got a message, but he wasn't specific."

"Well, how do you feel about making a quick trip out to check on Robert?"

Reva thought for a minute. After all the dreams she'd had about Robert lately, she felt like fate was weighing down on her. She counted in her head, *It's been sixteen months since I last saw him. He could be healed by now.* She fought a breathless excitement at the thought, but calmly answered Stan, "Well, sure. Is it safe to go find him, I mean is he still in a safe house in Boise?"

"Actually, he's spent the winter with Mitch and Jenny in Utah. Jonesey wonders if he can use him in Boise or Phoenix this summer while we continue waiting for the Renata money to dry up."

"Ok, but why does Jonesey need me?" Reva asked, hoping she could live with the answer.

"Well...both Jonesey and Mitch think Robert has improved, but both have told me that they are not sure Robert isn't hiding the truth from them...like he *seems* okay and gives all the right answers, but they don't want to rush him. On one hand it's been nearly three years since the torture, but on the other hand, Robert's life has turned a corner since then. I'd like you to spend up to six weeks there, to evaluate him. If you think he can be a good agent for us here in DC, I want to know. I also want to see if he'd give you an honest answer about his plans."

"Ok, Stan. I think I can do that. When do you want me there?"
***

Stan smiled, he'd heard from Jonesey about something brewing between his two orphan team members, and he wanted to see if he could rattle Reva into admitting something. "Let's say next week at the latest. Can you go today or do you want to wait and go next Tuesday?" Stan laughed at the look Reva gave. "You look shocked. You know me, why wait when I can do it now. I know the Renata trials are on hold until next month, so you have time."

***

Reva tried to control the blush at the thought she might see Robert within a few hours. She swallowed, and acted cool, "Doesn't matter to me. I'm open."

Stan nodded, "Great. I'll tap Denise and see when she can get you on a flight. Hang out at your desk for about twenty minutes."

"Ok, boss. Talk to you in a few." Reva turned away and headed back to her office.

Reva sat at her desk and thought about her upcoming weekend plans. With all her family now in Israel, she usually only had plans when her friends had a party or a life event. The rest of her time, she spent puttering in her condo or driving around. She'd also worked hard to forget that yesterday was her thirty-ninth birthday.

Mentally, she considered the best plans for a quick trip to Salt Lake City. Because she was usually undercover on assignment, Reva had a startling array of clothing here in the locker room, including an emergency travel kit. She reviewed her wardrobe mentally and decided she could make it to Utah directly from here in the office. Her condo would be fine without her, all the plants were silk, and her garage was secure. The security system would keep the lights going and she could monitor things from her phone.

"I could go downstairs, pack a bag and head straight to the airport," she thought, and then Stan's secretary Denise buzzed her.

"Reva, Stan asked me to call you before I made the final reservations. There's a flight going to LAX with a connection back to SLC that leaves tonight at eight, or there's a four-o'clock flight to Denver that has a few SLC connections. Can you leave now?"

Reva went with her impulses. "Yes, I can be downstairs in ten minutes."

"Good. I'll get you on the four-o'clock flight. Stan has a voucher with the airline, so you'll be in first class, and I'll have a driver downstairs in ten minutes. Bye."

"Bye."

In twenty minutes the driver had Reva well on the way to the airport. They were barely ahead of the rush hour, but being a holiday weekend, traffic was light, as if folks were already gone from the city. Reva's face glowed with her excitement. *Whatever happens, I would love to see Jenny and maybe we can go shopping tomorrow. Salt Lake doesn't have the big shopping I can get out here, but I can't shop with Jenny here. She always steers me to my best outfits; even if I have doubts, she has a better eye than Mom and makes me feel like a fashion plate.*

Reva clutched the sleek leather overnight bag, which she'd successfully filled from her office stash, as she dialed Jenny's number. "Sure, Jenny, I can catch the train. See you in Ogden at the FrontRunner station at ten your time. Bye."

Reva was excited. She'd worried about driving from Salt Lake to Ogden, as much as she'd worried over making Jenny or Mitch drive down to Salt Lake from Ogden to get her. She had driven to Jenny's house once before, but wasn't sure she could find it again in the dark. Also, she didn't want to put out either Mitch or Jenny by having them come and get her, and she hated airport shuttle vans. She loved DC's metro and was excited when Jenny told her that she could take Salt Lake's light rail system to the high speed train that ran between Ogden and Salt Lake. She couldn't wait to get to the airport. She'd see Jenny (and maybe Robert) tonight!

Chapter Sixteen
Reva's Coming to Utah

Jenny looked up from her perch at the kitchen table as Robert came upstairs. She'd just hung up the phone with Reva and looked at him speculatively. Robert didn't notice as he came over and gestured for the phone in her hand.

"Is it okay if I call Stan? He emailed me and asked me to call him. Something about the Renata trials."

"Of course. Do you need me to step out?"

"No Jen, I may need your advice, so hang out for a while."

Jenny went back to balancing her checkbook, so she could have it done before the kids got home in an hour. *I hope Mitch can spare a few bennies [$100 bills]. I'm sure Reva will want to go shopping.* Jenny paid as much attention to her bank balance as she could while actively eavesdropping on Robert's call. As he got going, she wished she had the balls to pick up the extension to hear Stan's side.

"Hey, Stan. You sent an email about the Renata trials?"

"So they really want to see me as much as they want me to testify."

"It's the last Renata brother?"

"Ok. DC on March 1. I'll try."

Robert hung up the phone, and looked at Jenny, "Can you guys watch Sam while I'm in DC for a couple of weeks?"

"Of course. Will you be okay?" Jenny stood up and came over to Robert, her face full of concern.

"I think so. I mean it's been nearly three years and the Renata brothers I knew are dead, while the rest are in custody. I should be ok."

"Well, I think you should talk it over with Mitch or Jonesey before you make your final decision. Besides, maybe you should take Sam with you. They do have service dogs in DC, and he could take a bite out of any assassin that got too close."

Robert laughed at Jenny's joke.

Jenny turned back to the table. "Oh, hey, Robert, can you do me a favor?"

"Sure, what?"

"Sounds like Reva is coming out tonight to meet with Jonesey. Her flight hits Salt Lake at nine. Can you pick her up at the FrontRunner station at ten?" Robert's jaw dropped for a second. Jenny watched him. She imagined she could actually see his thoughts. *Jonesey was right. He does have a case for her. So much the better.* Jenny smiled, and asked innocently, pretending she hadn't noticed Robert's pause, "So can you? I could, but it will take me some time to make up a bed for her."

"No, no. I can go. She's coming up on the FrontRunner?"

"Yes, at 10."

"Ok. I'll get her."

"Great."

Jenny watched Robert walk out of the kitchen. *He looks a bit blind-sided. I can't wait to see the two of them together. Amy and Jonesey have their suspicions, but I'll need to see Miss Reva and him together for myself. If she does like him, it's about time.* Jenny sighed and smiled and went back to her bookkeeping. *Any matchmaking can wait.*

Chapter Seventeen
Reva and Robert in Ogden

Robert parked his Jeep as close to the FrontRunner stop as possible. Being a Friday night on a holiday weekend and despite a recent snowstorm the lot was mostly full. Thankfully the walkways were clear of snow. He wondered absently whether or not Reva brought a coat. Winters were as cold in DC as they were in Utah, but not usually as snowy. Mitch was excited to see Reva. He'd said as much once he'd gotten home and heard the news, but Robert was suspicious. He'd caught the look that Mitch had sent Jenny. *I bet there have been some calls out here from Stan, especially if Jonesey shows up on Sunday as planned. Oh well, whatever they have planned for me I am ready.*

Robert hadn't realized it until he'd had the thought, but he *was* ready for his FBI life to start again. He'd known how Stan operated, and he could just see him sending Reva out to measure his progress in terms of his FBI feasibility. "Well I am as ready as I will ever be. Besides, it could just be that she's coming out here to prep me for the trial next month."

Robert looked at the Jeep's clock. 9:40 PM. The Harper kids were in bed, but Mitch and Jenny were holding a late supper for Reva. *The train should be pulling in any minute.* Robert looked at Sam.

Sam looked back at him, tongue lolling out, woofing as if to ask a question.

"You're right buddy, let's get out and wander around as we wait."

Sam barked as if to say "Yes, let's."

Robert hopped out of the driver's seat and opened the rear door. Sam jumped down and they played a bit before taking the walk down to the gates where FrontRunner passengers disembarked from the high-speed commuter train.

Robert focused on stretching his left leg. He could never stay still for long without having it spasm even now. Walking around was the best way to keep it loose and limber. He let out Sam's lead to the maximum length as they strode around the lot.

Soon enough the huge white train with bright blue and red markings pulled into the Ogden Transfer Station. Robert noticed many cars running to stay warm while other folks waited for the train, as well as a handful of local transit buses. The FrontRunner came once an hour to bring folks north to Ogden from points south, but mostly Salt Lake City. The Utah Transit Authority (UTA) had only recently opened the light rail line between Salt Lake City proper and the Salt Lake City international airport. Robert enjoyed people watching folks getting off the train. There were a few air travelers, marked by their rolling luggage, but there were more young kids clearly coming from or to a party here in Ogden. *Lots of millennials these days.* Robert thought as he watched a young couple in tight jeans that rode low with multiple piercings, both wearing backpacks and sharing a set of white ear buds as they walked in sync. *Old Joe McCarthy would have kittens watching the millennials—these twenty-somethings are little socialists.* He thought humorously.

Just past the couple, he spotted a pair of long legs in a short black skirt, knee-high boots, and black tights. A gray tweed fitted coat with a wide skirt came into view, but it the bright rusty-orange scarf caught his eye. Sure enough it was Reva. He saw that she'd tamed her reddish-brown curls into a tight knot, but had a swooping lock across her forehead. He raised his hand in the air. She saw him and waved back.

Robert stood and just drank in her appearance as he let her approach him. *Leave it to Reva to travel in high style,* he thought as he watched her half-turn to ensure that her ox-blood leather case was rolling along behind her properly.

It had been almost a year and a half since he'd seen her and she looked better than ever. The tights and tight boots emphasized her long, slender legs and calves, while the fitted and flared coat showed off her tiny waist. The scarf set off her hair and he couldn't wait until she came closer and he could stare at her amazing eyes. *Thank you, Lord for letting me see her once again.* Robert's prayer was sincere. He no longer took anything for granted; including the chance that he'd meet Reva once again. *I'm not fully healed yet, but at least I can walk this time.*

***

Reva had fallen asleep on the train. The jet lag was catching up with her. It was around midnight her time, and she'd been traveling since she'd left the office at three. *Thank heavens Denise found me a quick way to get here. That last flight from Denver took only forty-five minutes.* She'd hoped she'd brought enough warm clothes for a Utah winter, and was glad the wooly tights and leather boots kept her legs warm. She had found the military-cut ladies coat in her work wardrobe and was glad to have a warm scarf for her neck. The thought, *No gloves though. I'll have to ask Jenny for a pair.* made it through her head and then all her thoughts quieted as she looked down past her fellow passengers. She'd spotted the golden German shepherd first. Then she'd followed the leash to a very tall man. It was Robert.

He looks good. He's standing straight, and the hair's grown a bit. I like the long hair on him. Makes him look like a pirate out of a romance novel and less like an FBI agent. Robert raised his hand in greeting and she waved back. As she tugged her case towards her ride, Reva felt a wave of expectation wash over her. She was so happy to see Robert again and to see him looking healthy was amazing. *Thank you, God for sparing him, and for letting him walk again. Amen.*

***

Reva was all smiles as she reached Robert. He held out his hand to shake hers, but she dropped her case handle and slapped his hand down. Before he could register her intent, Reva moved in close and grabbed him in a big hug. He slipped his arms around her automatically and tried not to die at the pleasure he experienced holding her against him.

Reva squeezed his waist as she spoke near his neck. "I am SO glad you are doing so well. I hoped I'd get to see you up and about on two legs, and here you are." She squeezed again and then released him and backed away. "Thank you for meeting me. I wondered who would come down, but I am glad to see you!"

"Miss Reva, you look good enough to eat. Look at you, practically right out of a fashion magazine. I bet you caught everyone's eye in the airport."

"Sure did. Stan used his vouchers and got me upgraded to first class the whole way. Everyone was looking at me like I was a movie star."

"I believe it."

Robert reached past her to grasp her case trying not to notice how well she fit next to him. Reva watched him and then remarked to Sam, "So Robert is this your dog, Sam?"

"Sure is. Sam, say hi to the lady."

Sam recognized his master's command and moved forward and then sat on his haunches at Reva's feet.

Reva held out her hand, fingers down to let the dog sniff her. He politely licked her fingers once and then sat back wagging his tail.

"What a sweetie. You're a lucky man, Robert."

"Thank you. I agree. Sam lost his police officer to come to me, so it's a mutually beneficial arrangement. You're right, though. He's a real blessing." Robert transferred Reva's case's pull handle to his leash hand and grasped her elbow with his other hand. "My lady, your carriage awaits. This way."

They walked side by side with Sam and the case following to his Jeep. "Oh. Jonesey told me about your Jeep, but it's better than I pictured."

Robert smiled as Reva moved in closer to inspect the tread on his off-road tires and then stand on tiptoe to look at the roof rack. He sighed. *This woman is just too sexy for my piece of mind. Crazy about cars, wears great clothes and hugs instead of shaking hands. Damn, short skirts and high boots should be outlawed. I wonder if Reva knew how that skirt would ride up the back of her thighs and show off her legs. She's worked undercover a long time. I bet she knows just exactly how sexy she looks tonight.*

Robert came up behind Reva and reached past her to open the Jeep's rear passenger door. "In you go, Sam." He said as he unclipped the leash. Sam gracefully jumped up and moved to sit in the middle of the bench. Robert stowed Reva's tiny rolling suitcase on the floor behind her seat before opening the passenger door and handing her into the 4X4. *I'll remember the way she scooted onto the seat butt-first and then swiveled her legs in for the rest of my days.* Robert thought as he crossed in front of the Jeep to his own door. *Please Lord; don't let me screw this up.* Was the only thought in his head as he headed home to the Harpers'.

Chapter Eighteen
Jonesey Comes for Sunday Dinner

"So Robert, are you going back to DC to testify?" Jonesey asked across the Harper's table. He and Reva had joined Robert and the Harpers for Sunday dinner.

"I think so. Reva said the hit has been called off, now that we have successfully frozen all the Renata accounts. They don't have the cash to pay off a hired hit man and we have all their known guns in custody."

"That matches what my sources say." Mitch added. The talk turned back to Reva and Jenny's shopping trips, the one yesterday and the one planned tomorrow.

Robert covertly watched Reva as she and Jenny talked animatedly. He looked over and caught Jonesey watching him watch Reva. He looked across the table and saw Mitch doing the same. He raised his eyebrows to both agents. *What do I care if those two know I'm fixated on Reva. Heck, it may help. Maybe they can fill me in.*

Jonesey shook his head and turned back to Jenny to ask her a question. Mitch focused on his food, but grabbed Jenny's hand to hold it as he ate.

Reva remarked, "Mitch, if you hold Jenny's right hand, she won't be able to eat."

"Reva, if you haven't noticed, my wife hasn't stopped talking since you got here. And since she talks with her hands, I can keep her from talking when I keep them from moving. I swear she hasn't ate anything yet for all your yapping, her mouth's moving too fast." Jenny snatched her hand away, and Robert could swear she kicked Mitch under the table, because he winced.

Jenny spoke up. "Sorry everyone, it's just been so long since Reva and I have been together."

"Jenny, ignore those two. You're fine as you are. Eat or talk, as you like. I for one am enjoying a happy meal here." Jonesey punctuated his opinion by stabbing a piece of asparagus on his plate.

To change the subject, Robert asked, "So Reva, are you really here to interview me for Stan?" Jenny and Mitch jerked, apparently shocked at his boldness.

Reva just smiled. "You got it, Robert. Stan called me out here to form my own opinion of you and your status because he's not sure you'd level with Mitch or Jonesey here."

Robert laughed, "My heavens, that's great. I bet you two didn't even know about it either." He looked at Jonesey and Mitch who both shook their heads. "I guess it's my own fault. I told you guys how I was doing when you asked, but I haven't called Stan yet."

Reva interrupted him, "You don't need to. Stan was fairly sure of your status based on Jonesey and Mitch's reports, he just wanted my take on things."

Jonesey muttered, "I wonder." Quietly, but both Reva and Jenny heard him.

Jenny spoke first, "What do you mean, Jonesey? Why did Stan *really* send Reva out here?"

Jonesey looked at Reva and saw that she had a questioning look on her face to match Jenny's. He looked at Mitch, who shook his head at him. He then looked at Robert, who shrugged, obviously clueless. He looked at Mitch as he started to speak.

Mitch got out, "It's your head..." when Jenny cut him off.

"What is it that you and Jonesey know that the rest of us don't?"

Jonesey asked Mitch, "So, should I put it out there?"

Mitch shook his head and looked away, "It's your call. I wouldn't, but you know these two aren't going to give up until you spill now." Mitch gestured to Jenny and Reva.

"Fine." Jonesey met both Robert and Reva's eyes

and said, "Well, you both know that Stan was going to partner you, but he got a report that you two may be *too* well suited."

Robert narrowed his eyes and tightened his lips, fearing that he knew what Jonesey was going to say.

Reva still hadn't caught on, "What report and what do you mean by *too well suited*?"

Jonesey gave in, "Well hell, Caspar noticed some chemistry between you two back in the hospital and he told Stan. He wanted you out here to see whether you thought Robert is ready to come back to the FBI, but he *also* wanted Mitch and I to see you two together to see if you were into each other, ok." Jonesey couldn't take the pressure and walked away from the table, "Now you know. I need some air."

"Oh my GOD!" Reva exclaimed as she burst into hysterical laughter.

Jenny looked at her and started laughing too.

Mitch looked at the women and sighed. He stood up, and patted Robert on the shoulder as he headed to follow Jonesey. "Sorry, man. Good luck."

Once his buddies abandoned him, Robert decided he'd have to deal with this news. He'd known that he'd probably fallen in love with Reva months ago, but he'd figured he'd be stuck in his unrequited state. *At least it's out in the open.* He thought, as he stood up. He walked over to Jenny and pulled her out of the chair. "Go talk to Mitch and Jonesey. I need Reva for a minute." And he pushed Jenny out of the dining room.

Reva was sitting there staring at him, with a quirky smile on her face. Robert sighed and took Jenny's spot next to her.

Robert scooted the chair closer to Reva and angled it so he could face her head on. He reached down and clasped her right hand in both of his. "Reva, I am sorry to embarrass you. But, I have to admit you are the most beautiful woman I've ever met, which probably showed in the way I've watched you. I'm sorry to cause you discomfort." To his horror, Reva laughed again.

When she'd regained control, she spoke, "Oh Robert. That's the best thing I've heard in years. You are the most handsome man I've ever seen, and I nearly told Stan that I couldn't be your partner, because I was worried I would jump your bones." She dissolved into another laughing fit.

Robert just stared at her, "What's so funny? I don't get it. Aren't you embarrassed that everyone thinks we have a case for each other?"

Reva wiped the tears from her eyes. "Oh, no, Robert. I am way too old to be embarrassed about any feelings I have for someone. I am laughing, because both of us know better than this, we should have talked about this much sooner. I should have told you that I liked you before you left DC. We never should have had to have an intervention…"

Reva's words were cut off as a projectile shattered Mitch and Jenny's living room picture window, slicing past Robert's side and lodging in Reva's chest on her left side near her shoulder.

By the time the second shot followed, Robert had both he and Reva on the floor as they heard at least two guns return fire from the front porch. Robert pulled off his T-shirt with one hand as he lifted Reva's shirt with his right hand to see the wound. It was a through and through and she was bleeding heavily. He wadded the T-shirt over the exit wound under her, and then pressed her back down, holding pressure on the entrance wound. He switched holding the makeshift bandage from his right hand to his left, so he could grab his cell phone. He fumbled a bit and then successfully dialed 911. He heard Jonesey shouting to Mitch in the front yard.

"Mitch, get your rig! I got one of the rear tires.

Follow me so we can catch the bastards." Mitch then yelled to Jenny, "Call the cops. We'll be right back. When the cops get here, call Reggie so he can get the SLC FBI guys down here."

Robert's call went through, "Yes, operator. Shots fired. We're in an FBI safe house and one person is injured. Yes, a gunshot wound. Yes, we returned fire. Two agents are in pursuit of the vehicle, but I need a bus. The injured is a female agent. It's a through and through and there's too much blood." Robert gave Mitch's address as Jenny came in talking on Mitch's cell phone. Robert continued with his call, "Yes operator, another member of our team is also calling you. Can I turn you over to her?" He reached up to give Jenny his cell phone. She spoke to both operators in turn until blue and red lights shone on the ceiling indicating the Ogden Police Department had arrived.

Reva kept going in and out of consciousness while Robert kept up a chanting, "You'll be okay, Reva. Stay with me. You'll be okay. I got you. Stay with me, Reva…"

The ambulance arrived a few minutes later and Robert followed Reva's gurney into the back of the ambulance as Reggie, the head of the Salt Lake City (SLC) FBI office who lived just south of Ogden arrived.

"Leland, where's Mitch?" Reggie asked.

"Him and Jonesey took off after the shooter. Jenny's inside and may know more. I'm going with Reva."

Reggie clapped him on his shoulder and handed him a holster. "Take my piece. We just got word. They think it was the Renatas—they must have followed Reva out here. Take care of yourself."

At that moment, Jenny tossed him a new shirt from the drive, "Go, Robert, we're fine now that Reggie's here. Keep Reva safe."

Robert shrugged into the shirt thinking, *Heck. I didn't even notice I am outside half-naked in winter.*

An hour later, Robert sat in the family's waiting

room at Ogden's McKay-Dee hospital waiting for Reva to get out of surgery. As he sat, he fingered the gun Reggie had given him. A woman in scrubs knocked on the door.

"Mr. Leland?"

Robert looked up and nodded.

"Reva is going to be just fine. They were able to stop the bleeding, but need to work on some tissue repair. She should be in recovery within a couple of hours."

"Ok. Thank you." Relief flooded Robert. "Thank you, Heavenly Father. Thank you in Jesus's name for saving her."

"Robert?" Robert looked up to see Jonesey in the doorway. "It's time for you to go."

"What? I am waiting for Reva."

"No time. It was the Renatas. They had a perfect shot into the house with the lights on, but it was an amateur shooter, a cousin or somebody. We caught him after he ditched the car in a park, but you need to go now. The Renatas are going to keep coming now they've found you using whatever friends and family they can now we've cut off their funds. Mitch and Jenny are going into hiding with the kids, and I'll take care of Reva, but you need to go with the US Marshalls NOW." Jonesey came over and pulled him up. He took Reggie's gun and handed him another in a holster. "Here's your gun from my storage. The rest of your kit is in here." Jonesey gestured to a duffel. "I'll have Sam with me. Get through the trial and then I'll come for you." Jonesey put the duffel into his other hand and pulled him out into the hall. "This is Cope. He's one of the US Marshalls stationed out of Salt Lake. He'll get you to DC in time for the trial. Until then, Vaya Con Dios."

Numbness overtook Robert. He heard Jonesey through a fog. He'd never be free of the Renatas, and now they'd not only nearly killed him, but Reva too. He barely registered leaving the hospital or the marshal driving him out of Ogden. At some point he must have slept, because when woke, he was laying in the back of an unmarked police car in Four Corners, on his way to Albuquerque, NM.

Chapter Nineteen
Renata Trials Over

"I am so glad the trials are over." Jenny remarked to Mitch. Stan had called with the good news that morning. They had won the last case and all the Renata players were behind bars. The crime family was finished. All their assets had been seized and all the remaining male family members down to age fourteen had been indicted and convicted. "Robert will be free now, won't he?" Jenny asked.

"I think so, especially if he stays out here."

"Have you heard from Jonesey yet? Will he bring him back here, and Sam too?"

Mitch looked down at his wife. In the six months since the Renatas had shot up his house, the world had changed once again. Jenny absently turned away to look back at her new picture window—bulletproof glass this time, she'd insisted.

Jenny asked, "I wonder how Reva is doing?"

Mitch sighed, "Well she's been out of hiding for a couple of months, but Stan is keeping her close to home."

"Good, I think I'll call her."

Mitch watched his wife wander back into the kitchen. She looked tired, and he'd caught her throwing up this morning. He was beginning to suspect Jenny was pregnant. He was concerned over this possible pregnancy. Not only had they thought they were done after Conner's birth, which had been nearly ten years ago. Jenny was now thirty-nine, and he worried about how another pregnancy would affect her body at this age.

Mitch's thoughts turned to Robert. He hadn't seen him since that night, but Jonesey had, and all he would say was that Robert was 'poorly'. Jonesey had stated the Marshals had kept Robert deep in the South West until the last of the Renata trials started and then kept him in a safe house in Baltimore throughout. Stan had alerted Mitch about Robert's status so he could prepare a home for him here in Ogden. Stan didn't mention Reva at all. That worried Mitch. *I wonder if Reva is ok. It's not like Stan to not talk about her. It's too bad things blew up before Reva and Robert could connect.*

Mitch wandered into the kitchen looking for Jenny, but she was gone. He went through the house looking for her. He saw his kids in the back yard. Danny was working on a woodshop project in the shed, Lisette was reading in the hammock and his youngest were up in the tree house playing pirates. But, no Jenny. Scowling, Mitch went upstairs and heard retching in the master bath. *Damn. If she doesn't stop throwing up, I am going to have to take her to the hospital for some intravenous nourishment.*

Mitch leaned against the door jam watching Jenny throw up. He walked over to hold her hair up away from the bowl and asked, "How far along are you?"

"Oh God. Not now, Mitch."

Mitch sighed and waited until she was finished. He helped her up and noticed how hot and flushed she looked. "Here let me." Mitch bundled Jenny's hair into a loose ponytail off her neck and then when he saw how hot she looked, stripped off her shirt so she was just in her underwear. He then wetted a washcloth with cold water and sponged her face and neck. "Do you want to drink some cold water or rinse your mouth?"

Jenny shook her head. "I just need to lay somewhere cool."

"Well, now that the sun has moved overhead, the back boys' room is in the shade. Can I crank up the AC for you?"

"That sounds good." Mitch led Jenny through their west-facing bedroom to Henry and Conner's east-facing room. He swiped a sheet from the hall linen closet in passing and laid it out on the wood floor. Gently he lowered Jenny to the sheet where she stretched out. He grabbed Henry's pillow and left to lower the temperature on their air conditioner.

The fans came on and a cool breeze hit Jenny from the hall.

Mitch came back upstairs with some mango ice cream. "You look cooler." He remarked.

Jenny didn't move, but answered, "This is the first time I've felt cool outside a car in two weeks."

"I bet. So do you want some of this?"

Jenny turned her face into the pillow. "Heaven's no. Mangos make me throw up."

Mitch went back to eating. "So how far along are we?"

Jenny sighed. "Not sure, I think 3 months. I've missed two periods, but the nausea only started last week. I took a pregnancy test yesterday and it was positive. I was waiting to tell you until I'd gone to the doctor. I have a doctor's appointment on Monday. Jenny turned to look back at him, "Are you mad about it?"

Mitch laughed and sat down next to her on the floor. He held the cold bowl against Jenny's neck and she relaxed happily.

"Of course, I'm not mad - just surprised. I mean, it's not like we did anything deliberately since Conner to *not* get pregnant. I just figured we were done."

"I get you. I was sure we were done too, until the first morning I threw up. Then all I could think about was how Mom used to talk about the super fertility we women get just before the big M. I think we got caught in the last egg or something." Jenny sighed. "I don't know whether to be excited or horrified at being pregnant at thirty-nine. I think they'd even call it a geriatric pregnancy and that sounds awful."

"Well there's not much we can do about it for now except keep you healthy, and honestly, it's time we upgraded the truck, and we can certainly get a new car seat for the van."

"Yeah. You're right. It's not like we haven't been through this before. I would just feel better if I didn't feel so lousy."

Mitch finished his ice cream and asked, "So what sounds good to you?"

"Nothing really. I've been doing soda crackers for breakfast, but I'm tired of them. I wish Robert were here."

That surprised Mitch, "Why?"

"Well, if I am craving anything it's Robert's bread—you know his grandmother's recipe? I wake up dreaming of drizzling honey over it hot from the oven. I miss his baking, he makes the best bread."

Mitch took the opportunity to raise his number one concern, "So Jenny, speaking of Robert, do you think you could handle him living here and your being pregnant at the same time?"

Jenny snorted and looked at him, "Of course. Why? He's no trouble. We have a routine and he's usually a big help around here."

"Well I just don't want to over-burden you... Which reminds me, the last time you were pregnant you hated going back to work afterwards. I think our finances can take it if you want to finally quit and stay home with the kids. I can afford a new car payment if I don't have to buy daycare."

"That's a good thought. Let me think about it. I have enough years of service that my IRS retirement can stay in place, even if I quit. I just can't collect until sixty-three or sixty-seven, so that's no problem. Are you sure, Mitch? I'd dearly love to be a full-time homemaker."

"You know I've always said that it's your choice to work or not. We paid the house off last year, and you've been good saving your pay, so we have a nest egg. I'm okay if you are.

"I confess that I like the idea, but I'll decide after talking to the doctor."

"Good plan."

Mitch left Jenny to nap as he went downstairs with his dish. He dialed Stan's cellphone as he rummaged in the fridge for some meat to throw on the grill for dinner.

"Stan, it's Mitch. We're ready for Robert whenever you are ready to send him."

"Good to hear, Mitch. I'll get on it and let you know when and where."

Chapter Twenty
Robert Returns

Jonesey recited the facts for Amy before leaving to get Robert, "The Marshalls flew Robert into Boise from DC on July 4. Since then, he's spent the last two weeks in a halfway house getting his bearings back while waiting for me to bring him his Jeep, Sam, and his gear. I'll take him wherever he wants to go from there. He could choose here, the cabin up north, or Mitch's." He gave her a hug and then whistled to Sam as he got in Robert's Jeep.

Jonesey made good time getting to the halfway house across Boise. He came breezing into the common room of the halfway house looking for Robert, who was sitting staring off into space. Robert had turned to look when the common room door opened, but didn't seem to believe who he was seeing.

"Oh my God, is that you, Jonesey?"

"Sure is, man. I'm here to liberate you." Jonesey hid his shock well as he pulled Robert to his feet and grabbed him in bear hug. "Let's go. Where are your things?"

"Upstairs, I'll get…"

Jonesey cut him off, anxious to get Robert out of there, "No, go sit in the car with Sam. I'll get your stuff."

Jonesey placed the Jeep's keys into Robert's hand and closed his fingers around them. He then nudged Robert out the door and headed upstairs to Robert's room. He noted the RL on the closest door to the stairs and found Robert's bag mostly packed in the closet. He rifled all the shelves and drawers and packed everything else into the bag. Shouldering Robert's gun in its holster he left the room muttering, "Good riddance."

On the long ride to Jonesey's place outside of Boise, he and Robert talked a little. Mostly Jonesey watched him, while Robert mostly sat and petted Sam's head where it lay down on the console between the two front seats. Robert looked peaceful and almost relaxed if a bit haggard. Jonesey turned his focus to driving and silently prayed for Robert. He looked healthy in terms of weight and movement, but sick in terms of skin pallor and there were bags under his eyes. Jonesey's prayers matched Robert's, had he but known it. "Please Father, Help me help him."

Robert was praying something like, "Please Father, Help me be better. Let Jonesey help me. Let this be real. Let this be the end, please Father."

Jonesey watched Amy welcome Robert home. He saw she noticed Robert's pallor, but she made no mention of it. Instead she moved into nurturing mode and did everything to help him be comfortable. Slowly over the next few days, His color turned more healthy as his diet improved. Sam helped him sleep, so the dark circles also lessened.

A week later, Robert came downstairs to breakfast and announced he'd like to go back to the River of No Return cabin. Jonesey overrode Amy's silent protest with his eyes. He could see improvement in Robert due to Amy's comforting gestures, but he was betting Robert now needed a heavy dose of freedom mixed with independence.

As they made the two-hour drive to the wilderness, Robert spoke a little about his future plans and hopes. Jonesey waited for him to mention Reva, but he didn't. Jonesey resolved to shelf the 'Reva question' for later and took hope in the fact that Robert was actively planning his life. "You know I'll need to pull you out by Labor Day, so you have about five weeks."

"That should do it. I just need my own space and my own pace for a while. If the radio's still up, I'll call you when I am ready to come back."

"Sounds like a plan."

Jonesey left Robert with a month's worth of supplies, books, and batteries, but vowed to return in two weeks.

***

Robert relished his newfound or reclaimed freedom. Living on his own at the cabin was as good now as it had been a year and a half earlier. In fact, Sam made it better, because Sam was overjoyed to be back with Robert and loved to 'talk' with him.

Robert still had his dad's old boxing gear, because Jonesey had thoughtfully loaded it in the Jeep from Mitch's shed. He took great pleasure in hanging the bags up. He found he enjoyed his balance and pound routine even more with Sam. Sam learned fast not to bite the heavy bag, but Robert somehow awoke his police training, because as he parried with the big bag, Sam would guard his weaker side and help him in the 'attack'. Man and dog developed a rhythm that suited them and pummeled the poor heavy bag.

Robert revived his habits of chopping wood, trekking down to the river, and taking long hikes, but he expanded his activities to allow for some late afternoon water play. Sam loved playing in the river and developed a fishing habit that kept him in fresh protein. More than one sunny afternoon found both man and dog cavorting in the currents, and then returning to the cabin for a fish dinner.

Chapter Twenty-One
Robert Receives Visitors

Robert had lost all track of the days. One August morning he opened the cabin's front door when he'd heard a vehicle approach, and was shocked to see Jonesey in full tactical gear exit a large SUV full of other FBI agents similarly attired.

"Robert, sorry to break in on you like this, but keep your eyes and ears open."

"What happened?" Robert asked conscious that he was standing on the front porch covered only by the blanket from his camp bed.

"Some dude kidnapped a girl in San Diego and instead of taking off to Mexico, as everybody thought, he dragged her up here. One of my buddies on the sheriff's posse spotted them on a horseback ride a couple of ridges over." Jonesey handed Robert a sheaf of papers and a plastic bag holding a sock. "Since you and Sam are up here, maybe you can help. If you see this guy, try to save the girl. I talked the FBI chief who's up here from San Diego into giving you one of the girl's socks. I figure if you're bored, head towards the old spring trail and see if Sam can catch the girl's trail."

The SUV honked, and Jonesey pulled away. "Don't stress as we're on it, but if you see something call out on the radio. I'll be on the usual channel." Jonesey then hurried back to the SUV and it sped off.

Robert shook his head and looked down at Sam, "So, boy, do you feel like going on a wild goose chase today?"

Sam wagged his tail and barked a single 'woof' as if to say YES!

Robert laid out breakfast and sat absently eating as he went over the kidnapper's dossier. He studied both the guy's and the girl's faces committing them to memory. He read about how the man was a family friend, who the FBI suspected had killed the girl's mom and little brother in his house before setting it on fire and taking off with the girl. Robert shook his head, *It's always something like this. But, maybe I should try. If they're going to hunt through this 300-square mile wilderness I better do my part.*

Resigned to his duty, Robert got dressed and grabbed his own tactical gear. He suited up in his best boots, shouldered his pistol holster and added the rifle holster across his back. He grabbed a mini-pack for ammo, his night-vision goggles, and light rations and two canteens. He pulled the sock in its sack from his pocket and helped Sam identify the girl's scent, grateful that the trainer had included a good foundation in Sam's law enforcement training before turning the dog over to him. He resealed the sock and he and Sam headed out for a walk.

At the end of the long day a tired Robert and Sam trudged up the last hill to the cabin just after sunset. He weighed the pros of cons of heading back out with Sam after midnight, to see if they could spot the kidnapper's campsite using his night vision goggles'. But he only made it to within 100 yards of the cabin before his leg gave out.

He went down hard. "Damn. I should have kept the walking stick with me."

Sam hovered, worried. After a few minutes Robert tried to stand. He could do it, but barely. Time to get to the cabin and hope the solar-powered cooler had some ice left or kept one of his gel ice packs frozen. Desperate, Robert pulled out the rifle, ensure the safety was locked and used it lightly as a crutch, grateful for its tough construction. By grasping the barrel and letting the stock push against the ground, the gun gave him just enough support so he could put some weight on his left leg. As he went, Robert cursed his leg. *I hope it can recover in a couple of days like it did last time I overworked it.*

It was full dark before he reached the cabin. But

when he looked, he saw another vehicle parked by his jeep. Concerned for his safety, he flipped down the night vision scope and scanned the cabin and its surroundings. The scope showed the vehicle clearly. It was an older truck and the engine compartment gave a faint glow, where it was still warm from the drive up here. Robert looked at the truck again and although he couldn't tell the color, it looked familiar. *In fact. If I'm not mistaken, that looks just like Jenny's old truck with a shell on it.* Robert decided that his leg hurt too much to assume an enemy had invaded the cabin. He needed to get off his feet sooner rather than later.

Five minutes brought him to the truck's bumper. In the faint starlight he could just make out the Utah plate with the word TRUCKY. *Jenny's plate all right, I wonder what the hell Mitch is doing up here.* Robert made his way painfully up the two steps to the porch and dropped the pack against the rocker. Taking a breath he moved a step to get to the door, when it opened. He looked up expecting to see Mitch or maybe Jenny, but it was Reva. Shock opened his mouth, "What the hell are you doing here?"

"Heavens, Robert, are you okay? Get in and let me look at that leg."

Pain made Robert ornery and cranky. "Ouch woman. Move out of the way. I need my chair now!"

To which, Reva shot back as she backed into the cabin, "I'm moving. Get in here."

***

Reva could only stare at Robert as she and Sam watched his slow and painful progress to the cabin's single chair where he sat and then laid the rifle across the nearby table.

Reva waited and when he leaned back, stretched his leg out, and laid his head back closing his eyes, she moved over to the cooler she'd found earlier. Rifling through the supplies Jonesey had pressed on her the day before, she found one of the gel ice packs and hurried it over to Robert.

Carefully she held it on his thigh where she thought his worst wounds had been. Robert didn't lean forward or look at her, but his left hand came down and softly covered hers as he slid the pack down slightly closer to his knee. Still without looking at her, Robert lightly squeezed her fingers.

"Thanks, sorry I yelled at you."

"No problem, Robert, I understand. Truly I do. Sorry that I startled you."

Robert opened his eyes and looked at her. He raised his hand off hers and lightly ran his fingers down her cheek and cupped it gently. "It's good to see you, honey. I've just had a very long and bad day." He paused and then ran his thumb softly over her bottom lip, "By the way, I'm glad the Renatas didn't get you." He dropped his hand back to the ice pack and closed his eyes once again.

Reva fought hard to tamp down her emotions telling herself Robert's actions were only a sign of his pain and stepped away to putter around the cabin. First she retrieved the pack off the porch. Robert didn't protest or move much as she unbuckled the rifle harness and then his shoulder harness. He did look at her and lean forward to allow her to slide them off his shoulders. Reva turned away and checked the water boiling in the large coffeepot on the stove.

She said, "Probably warm enough," and moved to the pack to unpack it as best she could. Once she'd stowed his gear, she set out food and water for Sam and brought Robert a cold bottle of water she'd stored in the cooler.

Robert drank as he watched her take down the old fashioned tub he used to soak laundry in and put it down in front of the stove. He saw her pour some of the room temperature water from the washing tank into it, then add boiling water from the coffee pot .

Reva stuck her finger in the water experimentally, and quickly pulled it back out. "Ouch! Too hot." She poured a bit more cool water and checked the temperature again. "Just right." Reva then reached into her pocket and pulled out a wax paper packet. She tore it open and sprinkled some herbs into the bath. Soon an herbal, minty, soothing smell rose from the tub. Reva looked over to him. "Don't worry, no lavender." She then came over and knelt in front of Robert. Gently she pulled his right foot forward. Robert could only watch as she untied his boot and removed it and his sock. She then rolled a cuff on his pants.

"Hold on, I need to remove your left boot, ok?" She asked. He nodded. Once she had his other foot free, Reva dragged the tub over in front of Robert and gently placed his feet in it. She had a large hand towel in one hand and reached for the ice pack with the other. "I know this is an awful angle for your left leg, but this should help while keeping you modest."

Robert didn't know what she meant until she dunked the towel in the warm water soothing his tired feet and wrung the excess water out. She then placed the warm and wet towel directly on his leg where he'd had the pack. The warm water was a shock after the cold, and Robert jerked, but the warmth soon soothed the leg.

"The compress should help with any spasms." was all Reva said. Then she went out the front door, leaving Robert with his thoughts.

***

Sam finished his dinner and came to lie near Robert. Meanwhile Robert had drifted off in a fog of fragrant steam that soaked away his hurts. He must have drifted off, because at one point, he awoke to a cracking fire in the fireplace, and a cold towel on his leg and cooling water around his feet.

To his left he saw that Reva had left another towel for him. Carefully Robert lifted his right foot out of the water and used it to gently push the tub out away from him. *Now comes the real test. Can I move the left leg?* In the past, Robert would be down for three to four days in excruciating pain, until his leg settled back down. Gently and with trepidation, he began lifting his left foot out of the water. The thigh ached, but the muscles did not clench or spasm with the movement. Robert took heart and began bending over to dry his right foot as he kept his left foot extended. It hurt but within an enduring level when he brought the left foot in for drying.

Robert managed to stand and then moved around experimentally, Hanging the wet towel from his thigh and his drying towel on the chair back and turned the chair towards the fire. *Reva can sure build a good fire.* He thought absently. *Where is she? Where did she go?* Gingerly he walked to the cabin door after checking his watch. "Nine o'clock. Time for bed." He'd bet Jonesey would want him back out at five in the morning to look for that girl. Rubbing his thigh, Robert said, "Hell with Jonesey. He can wait a day or two for me to go back out."

He opened the door and stepped onto the porch. It had become a bright night. The moon had risen and lit the sky well this far from any man-made lights. He'd thought Reva had only stepped out to find the 'facilities' out back, but she should have been back in by now. Robert looked over to his Jeep. Jenny's truck was still there. Then he glanced down and there was Reva asleep in the rocker.

The moon showed trails on her cheeks. Robert wondered what they were, until he realized they were tracks from her tears.

"God, Reva. You're breaking my heart." He shook his head, *As if I needed proof that I love her, here it is. Her tears tear me up inside.* He reached down and put his arms around Reva.

She made a small sound but didn't fight him standing her up. When she slumped towards him, Robert took a deep breath and then grabbed her around the waist and under her knees and hefted her up. She swung higher than expected, because she wasn't very heavy in his arms. In fact Robert had no hard time carrying her into the cabin and depositing her on the camp bed despite his leg. She snuggled into his pillow and didn't wake up, so he gently tucked his extra wool blanket around her. Standing over her Robert watched her sleep for a minute and then headed out to use the facilities after he banked the fire for the night.

When he came back into the cabin he saw that Reva had turned over, but was still sleeping. He moved the tub over by the old cook stove where he could reuse the water for a bath in the morning, and then laid out the spare bedroll on the floor next to Reva in the camp bed.

The next morning a bright shaft of daylight shone in Robert's eyes waking him up. He blinked a few times trying to wake up before he realized that he must have overslept in order to see sunlight. Quickly he glanced over at the camp bed. Reva was gone, but she'd made the bed. He saw that she'd turned off his wind-up alarm clock and fed Sam. He got up aiming for the facilities and then he'd find Reva.

Outside Robert enjoyed the early morning chill. The sun was up, but it was still early and the night's coolness had not yet worn away. He glanced over and then looked again to verify his first look. Jenny's truck was gone.

"Where's Reva? Did she leave already?" Robert thought for a moment, "Did I imagine her here?" He looked down and he could still smell the herbs on his pants, "No she was here." Robert hurried through nature's call and then rushed back into the cabin for some sign from Reva. Over on the cooler he spotted it. Reva had left another herb packet on top of a folded piece of paper. She'd written on the back of one of the wanted posters showing the kidnapper.

Tears came to his eyes, as Robert read Reva's note. "Dear, Dear, Robert. I am so sorry, but Jonesey called me on my satellite phone shortly after midnight. They found the guy. He's dead and the girl's okay, but there's no female FBI agent here besides me and the guys have scared the girl. I have to help get her to Boise and then to the San Diego staff."

At that point Reva had scratched out something and her writing, when it started again, was a little more sloppy as if she was rushing to get the words down. "I didn't want to leave you, but maybe it's for the best. I hated waiting around for you in this empty cabin. I got so scared. When you got back and dropped the pack, I could have shot you I was so freaked out. Then you were so hurt. I can't live off the grid, but I don't want to make you come back to DC for me. Please be safe and happy. Maybe one day we can find a way to be together. Goodbye. R."

Robert succumbed to the anguish in his heart. *Damn the FBI. I nearly had her. If only they hadn't found the guy last night. I know that we could have got through any issues between us today. Oh God. Dear Heavenly Father, please help me survive this.* Resolutely Robert began packing his stuff in high gear.

Chapter Twenty-Two
Robert Washes Up in Ogden

Mitch sat on the couch with Jenny in the front room enjoying a rare date night off from the kids. Jenny's sister had taken them to see *Despicable Me 2* at the dollar theatre. Jenny was well and truly pregnant and at nearly five months along her feet had begun to swell each night. Jenny had them in Mitch's lap and he was gently massaging the swollen tissues and watching TV when Mitch's cell phone rang. It was Jonesey.

"Hey Jonesey, what's up?"

"Nothing much. Just calling to give you a heads up. Robert's on his way down to you."

"Ok do you know his ETA?"

"Well..." Jonesey paused, which set off Mitch's warning system.

"Jonesey, what's wrong?"

"Well nothing really, not that I can tell, but Robert seems to be in a bad way."

"What happened?"

"Well you know how we caught that San Diego guy who kidnapped the neighbor's daughter. Well, Reva came out to help us when we heard she was in my territory, and Reva was going to hang out with Robert until we found the girl. Turns out Robert took Sam out on a search the day Reva arrived and didn't get back 'til late, so they didn't get time to talk things out. I'd hoped they'd start up where we left off last February, but no luck."

Mitch heard Jonesey pause to take a drink before he continued, "I guess that Robert's leg was hurting him so they hit the sack early, but we ended up getting the guy that same day. So, I called Reva in the middle of the night and made her leave Robert to help me get the girl home safe to San Diego. My timing must have been bad, because Reva was upset when she got to me and wouldn't talk about

Robert and then he came tearing out of there about six hours later hot on her trail, but missed her. He won't talk about her either, and he made it clear that whatever's wrong is my fault. Reva took off after my call and left Robert some sort of note ending whatever they had." Jonesey paused, "Look Mitch I gotta go. I'll do what I can to get Reva fixed, but in the meantime Robert is royally pissed at me and on his way down to find refuge with you. Good luck."

Mitch sat thoughtfully after Jonesey disconnected. He knew that Jenny probably heard most of what Jonesey said through his phone's speaker. He reached over and handed Jenny her cell phone from the coffee table, "Did you hear that?"

Jenny sat up slightly to take the phone, "Most of it. Do you want me to call Reva or Robert?"

"Probably Reva. Robert won't talk on a phone while driving and I'm not sure he'd talk to either of us about Reva."

Jenny started scrolling through her contacts to Reva's phone number, when Mitch reached over and held her hand to stop her,

"Just a sec. I had a couple of thoughts. Is your sister Fran still working on her chimney?"

"Yes, why?"

"Well I know Robert is way handy and Fran has a lot of bedrooms in that old Victorian. I wonder if she'd take Robert in and trade him room and board for some light carpentry or masonry repair. If he could handle it, that is."

Jenny thought for a minute. "Maybe. Fran has broke up with her guy, again, and so she's feeling bored and lonely. I bet she'd give Robert all the pampering and privacy he could stand. Also, unless Robert has regressed his leg should allow him to work at least part-time wouldn't it?"

"I think so, but we'd better ask to be sure in case."

Jenny had another thought, "Brent may have some room in his house if Robert wants to live with a bachelor."

Mitch looked thoughtful. "Maybe. It could work, but with him working nights, I am not sure Brent would be up to having Robert puttering during the day."

Mitch made his decision. "Ok. Call Fran after Reva in case Robert is too ticked off to stay here. We'll use the fact that he can 'pay' for room and board with light home repairs to convince him to stay with her."

***

Robert arrived at Mitch and Jenny's at midnight. He let Sam out and sent him into the familiar back yard for a run, after he parked the Jeep in his old spot in the back. Robert noted that Jenny's truck wasn't back yet, but that a newer, possibly brand-new GMC crew cab truck was in its place. He saw the kitchen light come on and decided to go face his friends. He hadn't been back here since that night in February. As he mounted the side steps, he thought, *At least I know Reva's okay and that she survived the wound.*

***

"Robert, I am so glad you made in safe!" Jenny exclaimed as she embraced him.

Robert hugged her back, genuinely glad to hug her. Jenny was a better sister to him than his own blood sister.

Mitch shook his hand, "Jonesey told us you'd be down, so we waited up hoping to catch you."

Robert spoke, "I hope I didn't wake your kids."

Jenny responded. "No worries. The monsters are with auntie and staying the night at Granny's. It was their last summer movie night before school starts."

"I suppose Jonesey filled you in."

"On what?" Jenny asked innocently.

Robert looked at her, trying to decide if she was playing him.

"About Reva, perhaps?" Mitch answered, "Look. Jonesey just told us something happened between you and

Reva and that you were coming in pissed off. It's really none of our business, but we care about both you and Reva and would like to help if we can. If we can't, we'll back off and respect your privacy."

Robert seriously considered Mitch's words before he answered, "Ok. There's not much to tell. We didn't get enough time to talk together, and she left me a freaked out note when she took off to help Jonesey. There's nothing I can do about it until I see her again, so it's on hold for now."

Mitch looked down to Jenny who smiled at him, so he said, "We can live with that. In the meantime, come in, sit down. Have you eaten?"

Mitch and Robert sat in the kitchen chatting as Jenny gathered food for Robert. Robert was glad he didn't have to sit in the dining room at night with the light on so shooters could see him easily. He wasn't sure he could even go in that room at night. He still had nightmares of all the horrific events of the past few years, but when Reva was shot, it added a new nightmare to his list. One where he held a bleeding Reva in his arms until she died.

To distract himself Robert watched Jenny work. She was an efficient worker and there was something restful and homey for him in watching her efficient movements. As she moved, he noticed something different about her. She moved a little awkwardly and didn't bend over as easily. He thought about how Jenny felt in his arms and wondered whether she'd put on weight, then it hit him, "My God, Jenny you're preggers!"

Mitch started laughing. "I told you he'd notice, Jenny."

"Damn it, Robert. I was supposed to win the bet." Jenny exclaimed.

Mitch chimed in, "I bet Jenny a steak dinner that you'd notice her belly before bedtime. She bet you'd notice sometime tomorrow."

"Well, you shocked me either way. I thought you two were done having kids."

Jenny cut off Mitch's answer, "He'll tell you I am just way fertile this close to the big M, but I'm telling you, it was his switch to baggy undies that did me in. All of sudden his swimmers are cooler and they got me."

Everyone dissolved into laughter at Jenny's ridiculous explanation.

Robert recovered and asked, "So when are you due?"

Jenny answered, "Well we aren't sure, but the doctor thinks around Christmas."

"Wow Jenny, a baby for Christmas. Lucky you! Poor kid'll get stiffed on presents. He should get double, but you know he'll get half or some birthday presents in Christmas wrapping." Robert remarked.

Mitch answered, "I agree, but oh well. Maybe Jenny will go later and have a New Year's baby instead."

Robert found he fit back into the Harpers' routines as easily as he'd relearned to live in Jonesey's cabin, but he began to feel restless after about ten days. He'd watched Jenny and noticed the changes in her since her pregnancy. She'd quit her IRS job and was a full-time Mom now, but she tired easily and had less energy. Robert started helping her more with her chores, and began to worry about space. With five bedrooms, the Harper house worked perfectly now, but none of the kids' rooms were big enough for two kids, really. And, Robert began to believe that he was in the baby's space. If he weren't there, Mitch could enclose part of the rec room and make the needed sixth bedroom. Guilt began to weigh on Robert.

Then Robert received a letter from Stan. "Robert, I hope this letter finds you well. I look forward to a day in the near future when you can return to active service. Reva apprised me on your work with Jonesey to help find the missing girl, and it seems to me that you could come back to us at any time. There's no rush, but in the meantime, if you encounter Reva on your journey, please send her back to me. She's angry at me and upset, and I fear for her future. She's a tough woman, but her life feels heavy to her. I suspect she may come find you. If so, please let her know that I am worried about her, and would like her to call me. Once again, congratulations on your excellent recovery. The team sends their regards. – Stan."

Robert shook his head. He could understand that Stan would write, but he didn't know what he could do about Reva or even himself for that matter. He turned the letter over to Jenny, telling her, "Reva will probably show up here, if she tries to find me, that is. I think you better keep this."

The next evening, Robert approached Mitch after Jenny went to bed early.

"Hey Rob. What's up?"

"Well, I need some space before the snow flies. I'm feeling a bit hemmed in and I don't know what to do. It's too cold in Jonesey's cabin and I am not ready to return to Grand Junction. Is there somewhere else in Ogden where I can hang out?"

"I can think of a couple of options. Let me get back to you tomorrow, ok?"

The next day Mitch asked Jenny's brother for a favor and let Robert hang out at Weber State. Jenny's brother worked in one of the buildings high on the hill above Ogden and he agreed to keep on eye on Robert and help him as he could.

Chapter Twenty-Three
Homeless above Weber State

Self-consciously Robert waited for Jenny's brother to let him into Weber State's Science Lab building. He worked in facilities/maintenance and would let him into the building for his daily shower and shave each weeknight. Robert hated homeless shelters. He also hated using truck stops to clean up. He didn't fit in at either place. He was definitely anti-social enough for the shelters, but he wasn't hopeless enough. The truckers just looked at him funny. It was clear he didn't have a rig, so why was he showering in their territory.

He was grateful that Mitch had found a way for him to try living a more free lifestyle. Technically, he was living like a homeless person, but he had more support that other homeless. *Besides, my pension might not be enough to feed and house me.*

There was one thing he couldn't leave behind when roughing it. Sanitation. He hated not being able to clean up. Especially out west where there weren't that many streams, rivers, or ponds—and, it never rained enough to clean you. Here outside of Ogden, Mitch and Jenny both offered him the use of their house, but he declined. He knew that if he showed up at the Harpers too often, Jenny would find a way to make him stay with them.

Jealousy also kept him away from the Harpers. Lately it was hard to watch Mitch be so happy with Jenny and their four kids, plus Jenny's new, surprise pregnancy. He wanted that kind of love and family for himself. Damn that bitch, Amanda. If it wasn't for her, he'd be in the same position as both Mitch and Jonesey. In fact, all the other agents he'd worked with in the last ten years were settled with a partner and most had kids.

He deliberately didn't think of Reva, it hurt too much. Part of the reason he was avoiding staying with

Mitch and Jenny was so that he wouldn't see Reva if she showed up there. Besides he was living homeless to see if he could hack it in the real world in case he could no longer 'work'. There was a real chance his family would not let him back into the fold. If so, and he couldn't go back to DC and Stan to his old FBI job, he'd truly be homeless.

Robert knew Stan would have him committed or at least dragged back to DC for intensive therapy if he knew how he was living right now. One day back in DC, Robert had joked with Stan that he'd be better off living homeless than staying in the hospital. Stan's reaction had shocked him. Stan was convinced that if Robert chose to live homeless it was proof of some mental defect.

Robert sighed and hoped he could make it the few weeks left until October. Then, he may take Mitch up on his 'plan 2' to stay with Jenny's oldest sister Fran, work on her dilapidated chimney and do other odd jobs for her throughout the winter.

Chapter Twenty-Four
Sleeping above Weber State

Two weeks into his stay in Ogden as a homeless man, and Robert was getting the hang of it.

"Thank God for mountains and this freedom. Amen," Robert prayed out loud. "Thank God for these mountains." was a constant refrain in his head. These northern bits of his own mountain range were both alien and familiar to this weary soul. Growing up in the hills above Grand Junction, CO, the mountains of the eastern Rockies were inbred within him. "All those years living in the flat of Texas. I never should have left the west. Why did I torture myself living so long in the flat lands without mountains to keep me grounded?" Robert rolled over on the goose-down filled sleeping bag that was the foundation of his bedroll. Sam stood up and nosed him to see if he was okay. The cool of the evening had forced him to bed down early.

Below the hill the lights of the university were coming on in the dusk. Mosquitoes were coming out and the sky to the west blazed orange and purple in the sunset. Robert noticed the lights and rolled back over to block the glare through his eyelids. He noticed the sound of the mosquitoes outside the netting of his tiny but efficient shelter. He no longer cared about sunsets. Inherited cynicism from his mother swamped him. Robert wondered if he should be like her and think of sunsets in terms of how pollution gave them their colors.

Tonight, like every night for the past weeks, Robert would sleep on the hillside of the mountain directly above Weber State University in Ogden. But lately he'd begun dreaming the dreams of the damned. That is, little or no sleep around horrific nightmares and flashbacks, with a few scarce hours spent in oblivion. Of all the places he'd slept in the past eight months, this was the most successful spot so far. With a giant pine tree to provide structure and shade for his tent-like shelter, scrub oak below for privacy, and the help of Jenny's brother who helped him with 'hygienic concerns', Robert had found the perfect place for him. No walls to hold him captive, no female relatives to rail at him, no concerned buddies to fuss and be helpless around him, and no limits to his freedom. He got up and went down with the sun, because it suited him. He found food each day at the various shelters in town or scrounged around the university. Jenny and Mitch supplied the rest of his needs. If he could only sleep, his life would be perfect.

Being homeless also helped him heal the mental wounds that had reopened during his six-month stint in protected custody with the US Marshalls during the Renata trials. During that time, he had no freedom. He couldn't drive, cook or leave their sight. Bathrooms became his only privacy, and his nightmares had returned full force the minute he'd been pried away from Reva in the hospital after that February night.

He blessed Jenny again for this spot. Then he did the same for her bother, who continued to let him into the science lab building so he could shower and use the restrooms as if he were a student or professor. He'd also drive Robert around now and then, especially down to see Jenny or Mitch.

Robert considered getting his Jeep from Jenny's house and decided against it. He'd have to have gas, and he'd be tempted to live in it. Better he stayed using his two feet for now.

Of all the agents' wives he'd met, Jenny most impressed Robert with her understanding of men. *She knows how men think, what they want, and how to take care of them.* Jonesey's wife, Amy looked too much like his ex, and most of the other agents' wives were too caught up in themselves to take note of some poor bastard 'let go from the agency due to mental issues.' Jenny's mercy felt like just plain old help, no strings, no lectures, and no costs unlike the strife he had to pay whenever he'd been near his mother or sister in the past. Just thinking of their harping about what he should do to get back into shape caused his stomach to clench and grumble with nervous anxiety.

On really bad days, he would think of Reva. He missed her. When they'd started talking in the hospital and became friends, he'd realized he could talk to her about anything. The few times he'd seen her since then, he'd grown more and more attached to her.

Maybe I should *go back to Mitch and Jenny's? I can sleep on the floor of the baby's room.* He was grateful he'd gotten to know Mitch. He didn't pity Robert or act uncomfortable, and was the only FBI buddy Robert had who didn't care what he did with himself, only that he found a better place to be.

If he went back, the Harpers would suck him back into their family. He thought about Jenny and wondered what living with Reva would be like. Jenny had given him a clean and cozy bedroom in the basement next to the furnace that was quiet and dark, but had sliding glass doors leading out to the back yard that allowed freedom. She never pushed him, but gave him support for all options. In comparison, Amy had told him to shave his mountain man beard, but Jenny simply laid out grooming shears, a beard comb, and a razor, which let him choose whether to groom or nix.

Over his time with the Harpers, Robert noticed how some of his favorites foodstuffs appeared in the household larder even before Jenny had started to consult him about his grocery needs. Next to Mitch's energy drinks and Jenny's Dr. Pepper cans, bottles and cans of Sarsaparilla and 2-liter bottles of Dr. Pepper appeared. *She even bought the drink we both prefer in my size of bottle.*

Jenny also enjoyed cooking with him, especially so when he would bake bread. She understood his baking supported his love of this favorite comfort food from childhood. One night, she'd heard him restless downstairs and surprised him with a bowl of this bread, broken into bits and covered with cold milk, 'bread and milk' something he hadn't eaten since childhood. Jenny handed him the bowl and a spoon, smiled, and left to go back to bed - instinctively knowing what he needed.

Robert sighed, "If ever I get tangled up with a woman again, she's gonna have to be like or better than Jenny. Maybe it's a good thing I am never doing that again. A woman like that has got to be rare." He squelched any thought of Reva, but let a question of "I wonder if eating bread in milk is kosher?" slip through his head.

Robert snuggled deeper into his new bedroll. Mitch supplied him with some gear, so he could better enjoy this time. *Maybe I better plan on living on a mountain somewhere between Ogden and Grand Junction permanently. It would have to be somewhere like Ogden which has both the mountain man lifestyle and easy city living. Either way, there is a lot of freedom in this way of life of having no home to tie you down.* The note from Reva burned in his brain. 'I can't live off the grid'. Reva represented hearth and home and if he couldn't live with her, he may as well be homeless.

Robert reflected on the two things Jenny required before letting him leave her house: 1. He must let her brother help him when necessary and 2. He must bring her or send her his laundry weekly, no buts. Robert nearly died when Jenny demanded his bedding periodically to wash it too.

Mitch had just shaken his head and remarked, "The woman made me buy her a killer washer for her quilts. I haven't seen bedding that she can't wash. Last week, she washed her uncle's horse blanket in the 'wool' cycle and aired it out to dry down here for a week. Just hand her the sleeping bag and be glad for it."

When Robert watched Jenny put tennis balls in her dryer with his pillow to 'fluff it up' he decided to leave his laundry in the hands of a professional. He could admit now that it was nice to have fresh everything now and then. Dirt was an unavoidable enemy when living off the grid. *Since I hate living dirty and not having sanitation, I better figure out a way to live 'on the grid' soon. I just wish I could sleep. If I could sleep through the night, I might start feeling better. If I felt better, maybe I'd grow the necessary balls to track down Reva one last time.* That thought sent Robert to sleep.

The next morning changed Robert's life for the better. He'd had a nightmare or two, but the one where Reva bled out in his arms shifted into something new, and Robert felt the dream change while he was in it.

He could feel Reva in his arms on the floor, like she'd been that night in Jenny's dining room, but the feelings morphed into their night in Jonesey's cabin. Robert was on the floor in the spare bedroll, but Reva was there with him, not in the cabin bed. As he held her in the dream, all of a sudden, she was naked in his arms. He woke up mid-dream with the taste of Reva's lips in his mouth and the feel of her soft skin against his fingers and his body. And, to his horror and then to his joy, he realized that his manhood was fully engorged and he'd had his first wet dream in more than twenty years. Somehow, in the night, his impotence had disappeared. In shock he spoke to Sam, "I never thought I'd actually *need* Jenny to wash my bedroll." and laughed.

That incident turned Robert's focus. He was scared to hope the change could be permanent, and he wasn't sure he could deal with the consequences of having a functioning manhood given the sad state of his love life. But he couldn't help feeling relief and happiness at being a 'real man' - a whole man once again.

Despite his worry that the ending of his impotence

was only temporary, the returning of his manly functions helped Robert regain his confidence and he started looking at his life with more hope than ever. He was even grateful when he had a similar dream with the same results a day or so later.

Then one morning Robert decided that the homeless lifestyle wasn't really for him—not anymore. Sure he could do it. He'd easily lived up here without potable water or fire, but he'd had regular meals, clean clothes and bedding, and regular bathroom breaks when he wanted. "I guess I really am a domestic animal. Damn."

Soon after his decision to go back on the grid, the first winter storm caught Robert by surprise. This late September storm started as rain, but above 6,000 feet, it became snow. Without a fire, he was too cold and uncomfortable to stay living in the tent any longer. Robert packed his bedding for the first load, the gear for the second, and took the third load of his shelter canvas, ropes, and shovel, and headed down the mountain. He vowed, "The next time I do this, I need a cabin and a pot to piss in."

Jenny's brother, Brent, loaded the gear into his SUV without comment and drove him down to Mitch and Jenny's. They were pleased to have him back, and Jenny's face lit up with happiness when he asked, "Do you have time to trim my hair and beard before I shower?" Robert let the warmth of a comfortable house envelop him. He vowed to find a way to make a life like this for himself.

Chapter Twenty-Five
Reva Touches Base in Utah

Reva sipped her herbal tea and was glad for the sunny warmth of Jenny's newly-painted dining room. "I like the new colors, and I have no bad vibes sitting here." Reva then changed the subject, "I feel like a bad Jew for saying this, but I hate Tel Aviv." Reva made an Ugh sound. Jenny nodded and focused consciously on keeping quiet in order to let her good friend vent.

"You should have seen them. There's Mom in her element. She's living this *Exodus* lifestyle in the Promised Land and is immersing her grandchildren in the culture of being *true* Israelis. You'd think I'd sold my soul to the devil when I told her I was ready to go home." In a perfect imitation of her mother's accent, Reva continued, "Oyh, Reva, how can you break your mother's heart? Washington DC is no place for you. If you don't like Tel Aviv, why not go to Jerusalem? This is your home. Your father and I made a place for you here, with Artie and Mari. You would be such a good influence on little Esther. She worships you and here you go wanting to go back to America after all the years we saved to move the family to Israel."

Reva continued, "Then, I came out to see you and discovered how hard it is to eat kosher in the west." Reva sighed. "I don't know if I'll ever tell my mom, I'm considering stopping eating kosher…I am not sure I even want to go to temple anymore."

Jenny exclaimed, "Oh Reevs, don't do that. I know there's a good Jewish community here, we just need to find them. I can also make my crew eat kosher all the time. We can go through this whole kitchen and get new pots and pans if you want to use my house as a base. I think I can even find a local rabbi if needed. I know I can find kosher food too."

Reva smiled over Jenny's cooperative attitude and

shook her head. "Jenny, I love ya! You are the only one of my friends who even understands that food storage and the pots you use affect kosher. But, I can't take you up on the offer. I need to move on. I don't know where to go, now that I have six months away from work. Thank you again for Stan's letter to Robert. I called him yesterday, as promised. Stan told me to decide whether to retire or come back, and he promised I could have my FBI job back next year, but I don't know what to do. I'd probably still be in DC if my town house hadn't sold so quickly."

"So where will you go?"

"Well Jonesey told me I could spend some time in either Boise or Denver giving some female fight classes. But, he also hinted that he'd sic me on Robert."

Jenny sat up, "Reevs, did you really run out on him last August?"

Reva blushed and then became upset.

"Oh no, Reva, don't cry. You know that I'll have to cry with you."

"Jenny, it was so hard seeing him so hurt like that. You can't imagine. Plus it was horrible in that cabin. I drive for hours on these eerie empty dirt roads to this ancient cabin out in the open—it was so exposed you could see it for miles up on this bluff. And I spend all day doing what I can to occupy myself with no electricity or running water. Then it gets dark and I begin worrying that Robert will never get back and it's too dark to see much of anything inside or outside. I built a fire for comfort as well as light. I even wondered whether Robert was out somewhere lying wounded and bleeding. You don't know how bad he looked when Jonesey picked him up in Boise. Amy told me he looked gaunt and haunted. So I just wanted so bad to see him to make sure he's okay. Then I hear this loud thump on the porch. I think, 'it's a bear' and rush to get my gun, then I hear some muttering and think 'it must be Robert', so I holster my gun and open the door, and I scared him or something, he jumps and then yells at me for being there. Then I noticed he's using his rifle as a crutch and hobbling awfully. I helped him ice his leg, thankfully there's a solar powered cooler there, and then I made a warm herb bath using water I had to boil on an old iron stove, for his feet and his leg and then I couldn't take it anymore."

Reva looked down, and Jenny decided they were getting to the real problem.

"I don't think he was happy to see me, and he looked so hurt and tired and here I was bothering him, so I went out on the porch to think. After that I don't know what happened, apart that I fell asleep there in an old rocker. I must have cried myself to sleep. But, somehow I was asleep in Robert's bed when Jonesey called. I dreamt that Robert carried me into the cabin, which I am still not sure he could have done, but he must have, so I even stole his bed. Then, because Jonesey needed me, I just scribbled a note and left."

Reva brushed tears away from her eyes as she continued, "Besides I'm too old and worn out for Robert. He needs some sweet young thing to bring joy and happiness back into his life."

Jenny shot her down, "Reva knock it off. You are only forty—perfect for Robert. He's the same age as Mitch and I can tell you, the last thing he needs is some immature twenty-something who will treat him like dirt. If I were you, I'd fight for him. Face it; Robert is one very sexy man. I get the whole wounded warrior vibe, but he's also so skilled and utterly competent in what he does. He may be broken, but any red-blooded woman would love to be in his way when he snaps out of it. Besides, I think he'd be perfect for you too."

Reva looked up and Jenny spoke to reassure her as she went on, "Also, I doubt you bothered him at all. The Robert I know could have certainly carried you into the cabin and he probably gave up his bunk happily, he's that kind of man." Jenny snorted, "Like he'd make you sleep on the floor, really. He was so worried about you that he left right after you. Jonesey said he got to his house a mere six hours after you did. I bet he was on your tail the minute he woke up that morning." Jenny paused and waited for Reva to answer.

Reva considered her reply, "Well if you say he cares, maybe I will reach out to him. But Jenny, you are *so* pregnant. How do I know it's not just your hormones talking?"

***

Mitch came home from work and the Harper kids blew in the door around him. He stood in the kitchen staring at his wife and Reva chatting at the table. With one ear he listened to the kids' noises upstairs, and when he heard no contention, he entered the dining room.

"Hello ladies. Busy solving the world's problems?" he asked as he reached down to give Jenny a sound 'home from work', 'good to see you' kiss. After he straightened up, he let his curiosity out, "So, did I hear you guys mention Robert's name?"

Reva and Jenny looked at each other, and then Reva answered.

"Well yes, I am considering going to find him." Reva waved Stan's letter to Robert at Mitch. "See. Jenny gave me the letter, but Jonesey has already asked me to track down Robert. *He* said maybe that I could help him gauge or improve his fighting skills."

Mitch nodded, "I can see that. You're still one of the best trainers I know, but would Robert toss you on your ass like he should?"

Reva shook her head and sighed. "Why you guys always get sucked back into the 'poor little woman' attitude, I'll never know. I haven't decided I'd do it yet. I have a few months to kick around the states looking for somewhere to settle, if I leave DC. Heck, I haven't dealt with my Chevelle or all my stuff. I just left it all in storage and came out here. I'd welcome your input. I trust Jonesey, but you know how he's such a fixer. He hates to see folks not 'doing something' to fix their lives. I don't think he knows that Robert is moving at his own pace, and that's fine."

Mitch looked thoughtful, "You got a point, and though I know Jenny agrees with you, I think Robert needs a good kick in the ass."

Both girls' eyes opened wide and they looked at him, shocked.

"Hey, I think Robert is doing some things great, but he needs to face some things he's avoiding…that's all. For one, his anti-social behavior isn't good and I think if he can't be around his family, he should go somewhere else and start being with people. Especially now that the Renatas are neutralized and he can come out of hiding."

Reva looked frustrated, "So, how would me helping him relearn to fight help that?"

"Well, Reva, honestly, Robert doesn't spend time with anyone for long…not for more than a meal. He's been that way ever since the US Marshalls took off with him. I think if you could room with him, or spend most of each day with him, you'd give him some needed interpersonal support."

Reva's eyebrows rose, "As a roommate? Really?"

"Well you know what I mean. A totally platonic, 'another human in the house', lifestyle that would help him not feel alone, nor crowd him. You have to admit you're a great person to be on a long stakeout with, and Robert could use some serene and calm company in his life. I think you could provide that. Jenny and I have tried to help him, but he's too antsy to stay here for some reason."

Reva replied with a bit of sarcasm, "Platonic, huh. Are you trying to reverse-psychology me into hooking up with Robert like your wife is?"

"Oh God! No Reva, that's not what I meant at all." Mitch was genuinely shocked.

Jenny noticed and said, "See Reevs, he didn't even consider you two hooking up. Mitch was probably meaning that you should consider Stan's original plan to have you two be partners, you know, you help him through a rough patch like a good partner."

Mitch nodded, "Jenny's right. You know what it's like to lose a partner, plus Robert's body will never be the same. He's got good function, but he lost a lot—he probably remembers what it was like when he was a healthy eighteen-year-old, all-star football player, and compares that to how he can only walk now. Plus, I think you are one of the few FBI physical trainers I know with the skill to give Robert the lethal edge he's lost."

Reva replied, "You are probably right. Let me meditate on that. Besides I can do some recon on his family. They are the one unknown set of variables in Stan's book." Reva sighed, "Heaven knows Grand Junction is on the way to Denver if I take the I-70 route. I could look his family up and at least give Stan a picture of things at home before I make my big decision."

"Yeah, and knowing Stan, now that Robert could go back to DC, he may throw in some special assignment pay and help you extend your nest egg."

"That's true. I think he'd rather we both come back to his team in DC rather than both take off into retirement. I'll need to plot some things. Number one is wheels. I wanted to take the rental back tomorrow and fly to Denver."

Jenny interrupted, "You can have my old truck if you want. It runs great, and I'm sure Mitch would have no problem with you taking it, and you know how it runs since you took it to Idaho. A 4X4 will help you get to Robert, if he truly plans to head into the hills to his grandpa's cabin."

Mitch took to Jenny's idea with enthusiasm, "Jenny, that's a great idea. Reva, we'll sign over the title and you can use TRUCKY for basic transportation while you're out here. Heck, you can even use it to trade in on another truck if you'd like. Jenny has already gotten her new one, and we still have a couple of years to get a beater car for Danny to learn to drive."

Reva looked at her two good friends, "That's sweet. I think I'll do that. It will also help me decide whether I should go from a Chevelle into a truck."

***

Reva had left for Salt Lake City for a few days of exploration only thirty minutes before Jenny's brother brought Robert home to the Harper house.

Mitch noticed Brent and Robert getting out of the car and grabbed Jenny, "Do we tell Robert that Reva was just here or not?"

Jenny sighed, "Let me think about it, and I'll tell him if I get a good vibe, ok?"

Mitch looked uncertain for a second, "Were we right to lie to Reva about them hooking up?"

Jenny shook her head, "I hated doing it to her, but you saw how upset she was. I think if we had pushed the fact that he really likes her, she may have panicked."

The couple stood and watched Brent, Robert, and Sam come up the steps to the front door. Robert looked better and much happier. But, it never seemed a good time to mention Reva, so neither Mitch nor Jenny told him she'd just been there.

***

Robert spent the night at Mitch and Jenny's and hoped he'd like staying with Fran for the next couple of months. He liked the idea of hanging out with her. She was nearly 50, but still a vibrant woman. Plus, staying there would let Mitch and Jenny work on expanding their limited space. Jenny looked really pregnant and waddled more every day. Robert felt a keen anticipation. He had hopes and plans and he began to pray that he'd see Reva one more time.

In the middle of the night, he had the same cabin dream with Reva, but he woke in time to make it into the bathroom before things got messy. He figured he could explain soiled sheets to Mitch, but he really didn't want to explain them to Jenny. Robert laughed, as he contemplated living like a 12-year-old boy with no control over his body once again. He'd definitely have to see Fran's laundry situation.

Chapter Twenty-Six
Thank Heaven for Fran

The next day dawned cool, crisp, but sunny. There was a light coat of frost on his Jeep, but Robert was happy to be back in civilization as he cleared the ice from the windshield and then followed Jenny to Fran's house. In a week, it would be October, but he'd have a warm place to stay for another winter.

Fran's long, blonde hair was lighter than Jenny's, but more chicly styled. They looked like sisters, but Fran's eyes were a chocolate brown in contrast to Jenny's bright blue. Both were lookers. Robert had met Fran many times over the past year. She and Brent were Jenny's only siblings who lived in Ogden, so she saw them a lot. He knew Fran restored old houses as a side hobby to her real job of designing commercial buildings and public spaces.

Fran hugged Jenny and then him as they arrived, "Good to see you, Jen. You need to talk to Mom. You're way too big to be just six months along! Maybe the twin thing has finally caught you and Mitch."

Jenny still looked horrified as Fran turned to Robert, "You are looking hale and hearty Mr. Robert. Just what I need. Wait 'til you see this place."

Fran then addressed Sam, "You look like a very good dog, Sam. Yes, sniff my fingers to make sure I'm no threat." When Sam was decided, Fran turned to let them into her beckoning Victorian project house.

"Robert, Jenny told me you needed something to occupy your hands for the winter along with room and board." She gestured to the sweeping stairway and the two wide openings in the entry hall, "Well, as you can see, I have plenty of space, and a huge fridge, so room and board will be easy. Whether you'll want to take on the various carpentry and repair tasks is up to you."

The group went first into the main living area that

used to be the front parlor. A large brick chimney took up half of the back wall, but hunks of bricks were missing, and large canvases draped the area around the chimney to catch debris.

Fran sighed, "Well you can't see it from here, but the innards of this chimney have been repaired and it is ready to function. Its back wall warms the dining room directly behind. The mortar's poor, and the bricks were falling when I got here, but when the specialists had to clean out the poorly maintained chimney, they ended up having to chip out the original inner bricks and tiles. The vibrations compromised the remaining mortar." Fran turned back to Robert, "Mitch told me your grandpa was a mason and that you spent your teenage years trowel-in-hand. Do you think my bricks could be redone? If so, can you do it?"

Robert cocked his head and looked at the bricks. As Fran and Jenny watched him, he picked up a few to heft their weight and feel their integrity, then examined the chimney from all aspects. He went into the dining room to check the back side. "I'd have to take them all down, and then put them all back up." He turned to look at Fran, "Do you want to keep the same pattern?"

"Yes if possible. The herringbone in the middle matches the pattern in the tiles in the kitchen and some of the woodwork upstairs."

"Ok, but I think more bricks are missing. Do you have any others?"

Fran sighed with relief, "Sure do. There are piles of spare bricks in the downstairs coal cellar, and we contacted a local brickyard that not only makes new bricks but also salvages old ones. I have two more pallets of those and one half-pallet of reproduction ones. We used stronger, reproduction bricks for the chimney top on the roof."

Robert smiled, "Then yes, I think I can help. It will probably take me about two weeks, but since we're inside, I can take my time and let the snow flurry around outside."

Fran nodded, "That sounds great! I can't wait for you to get started, but you need to see the rest before your agree."

The tour continued. Fran had been in this house for a couple of years and a lot of the work was done. The wooden floors were in fine shape; she had already repaired and refinished them. There were a few spots where the twelve-inch baseboard's trim was worn away and would need replacing. A couple of stair treads were cracked and needed repair.

When the stairs and trim were fixed, Fran said she'd go through and repaper the walls and refinish all the trim as needed. The only other big job was some cabinet/carpentry upstairs. Fran wanted to build a freestanding combination of shelves and benches to run in the center of the old nursery to divide it and turn it into a dressing room.

"So Robert, besides the chimney down here, this house needs some simple repairs to the trim and the stairs, the closet shelves upstairs, and then paper hanging - if we get to that point this winter. Up for it?"

"Sure. It sounds like a fine way to spend this winter."

Robert and Fran got along swell. She worked sixty-hour weeks when one of her designing jobs was going, but worked at her own pace the rest of the time. Fran had taken a few months off since she'd finished redesigning a Salt Lake hospital's new cancer ward. Her next job would start in January and so she was excited about finishing the house while she finalized various designs for other bids.

Robert liked the back bedroom, converted from an added-on 'back porch' and moved into it. He tackled the woodwork first, so that Fran could do any staining or refinishing while he was working on the chimney.

Fran was happy to take over Robert's room and board and enjoyed working him through his domestic troubles in a similar fashion as Jenny did. They begin doing laundry together as neither wore enough clothes to justify a load apiece. And, while Fran loved to eat, she hated cooking and encouraged Robert to take over her modernized and amazing kitchen. He spent hours trying new recipes.

Robert found a lot in common with Fran and they got along well. Fran was still beautiful at fifty. Her eyes were brown like his, but her hair was long and straight and flowed around her. Because they both had a lot of free time, they worked out a routine that suited each other. Robert found her attractive, drawn to her like Jenny, although she was more restful and peaceful. He heard the music from her design studio wherever he worked, and timed his day so worked on bricks as she worked on her designs.

They talked about everything. Fran became the first person Robert talked to about his impotence since his shrink. He'd asked her why she never married, and she explained that she'd had a radical form of uterine cancer in her teens, then a hysterectomy at nineteen to save her life. Fran's mom and dad were supportive, and her siblings had stood with her, but she never felt like she could get married.

"I couldn't have babies, so I figured no man would want me. Then, when I was older, I met a man and fell in love." Fran stopped abruptly. "Sorry. I don't like to talk about Norman. We were together for a long time"

Robert remarked, "I heard Jenny and your other sisters talking about you and Norm at one family party." Fran nodded, "Yes. My family hates him. We've always been rocky. He's a successful builder out in California. We're taking a break for six months. He wants me to move to California, but I don't want to leave my jobs here in Utah. We had a big fight just before summer and split." Fran cleared her throat, "After that I thought we were over, but he called me last month. We agreed to try to reconcile, but he wants space until Christmas."

Fran looked sad, "The plan is for us to spend Christmas Eve together and then decide 'yay or nay' once and for all, unless he or I call it off before."

"Fran, I feel for you. It's hard when things come between you and the one you love. I'll be here for you if you need me."

"Thanks, Robert, I appreciate that. None of my family really understands. They think I am too focused on my career. They don't realize how hard it is to combine two-half centuries of baggage into one life. They think I should just drop everything and move to California and live in Norm's Malibu mansion."

***

Robert loved taking down the old chimney and putting it back together. Fran took pictures of the pattern for his reference, then shared her studio with him so he could plan the new chimney. He loaded heavy bags of mortar in his Jeep, and Jenny lent him her new truck for bigger loads. He spent a Saturday laying down a path of salvaged carpet from Fran's stash, along his wheelbarrow path through the house and all around the chimney to protect the floors if bricks fell. He began gently removing the bricks—then spent days chipping at them. Getting rid of the old mortar was tedious yet relaxing and helped him think. Fran and Robert gauged the passage of time by the ever-growing piles of cleaned bricks.

Robert dreamt of Reva now and then. He remembered their talks in the hospital, how she looked the night the Renatas shot her, and the times he'd seen her since. He was worried that he'd built the real woman into a fantasy that he'd never experience. On bad days, he was sure he was doomed to be alone.

He admitted to himself that part of the reason that he and Fran got along so well, was that both of them each considered their love lives on hold until they resolved their issues with the 'one I want'.

A few weeks passed, and Robert began rebuilding the chimney. He started on the back wall, because it was solid brick, and Fran hadn't decided what material she wanted to use for the front mantle. They planned out a schedule allowing him to have the back chimney finished by Thanksgiving, so the family could eat here; the front chimney done by Christmas, so she and Robert could hang stockings for Santa; and the trim finishing done by January, so that she only had wallpapering left to do when her big job started. Neither one admitted it, but both Robert and Fran believed their time would end at Christmas. Both knew that Fran would probably try again with her guy. They had a good thing, were okay that this life they currently shared was only temporary.

Fran teased Robert about her family, "You'd think they'd question you and I cohabitating, but NO, all my sisters do is razz me about Norman. It's like they're pretending you don't exist - or that we're siblings. I don't get it."

"Well, Fran, I wonder if they're avoiding the issue, because they don't want to think of you as a loose woman who installed a toy boy into her latest mansion."

They both laughed over that thought.

Chapter Twenty-Seven
Things Get Complicated

"Hey, Frannie, come see. I got the chimney done in here." Robert's excited voice pulled Fran into the dining room from her studio.

"Robert, that looks marvelous and I think better than it did the day it was first built. Thank you so much." Fran grabbed him for a celebratory hug. "I think I found a mantle for the front. Tell you what, if you want to celebrate tonight, I'll go out and get the mantle samples from the place I found and I'll grab some steaks for us while I'm out."

Fran had found a stonemason who specialized in rock counters who also made mantles. While out, she met with him and got samples of slate to compare with the original slate counters in the kitchen. She and Robert spent a few minutes deciding which color they liked best for the mantle, and then Fran headed back to the stonemason to make her order. While she was out again, Robert cleaned up the dining room and started dinner.

Over dinner their celebratory feelings charged the atmosphere in the dining room with their shared excitement. All of a sudden, their easy companionship flared into attraction. Fran looked at Robert and he stared back at her. She was dressed to the nines, as was her habit, and Robert had cleaned up and put on some slacks for dinner.

They both know that neither of them were in this for the long term, but both felt lonely and found solace in each other's company. It had been a long time since either's last courtship.

Robert left his seat and walked over to Fran and then they moved to her front room couch, holding hands. They let the fact they were lonely people carry them away. They sat quietly and stared out at the mountains in the twilight, sitting closely, and still holding hands.

Fran looked at him. Robert smiled and grasped her face gently by her cheeks and kissed her softly. The kiss deepened and both felt their feelings escalate. After a few minutes, Robert pulled back and rested his forehead against Fran's with his hands on her neck just below her ears. His thumbs made small circular motions under her chin, as he tried to catch his breath. Finally he spoke,

"Frannie, you're amazing, and I'd love nothing better than to take you upstairs and start our first night of love. I'd love more than anything to stay here and be your man, but I think we both know that it's not the right time for either of us."

Tears fell down Fran's cheeks as she nodded. "You're right. I didn't know how to say it, but you're right. We may be the right people for each other, but it is not the right time."

Robert pulled her close and nestled her against his chest. "Yeah. My mom always said 'the right person, the right time, and the right place."

Fran answered, "You mean like when Mormon parents talk about getting married in the temple?"

Robert nodded, "Yes, and both of us deserve that kind of life. Fran, give me a few months to find out whether my dream woman is real and whether I can be with her or not. If not, I'll come back to you as a whole man. I would marry you in a minute, and I'll take you to the temple if it's meant to be."

Fran sighed and said sadly, "You're right. I have to find out whether Norm is the one for me. If so, I owe it to him to wait. Besides I couldn't marry you freely without being done with Norm once and for all." Fran shook her head against Robert's neck. "I'll know by Christmas, and I can wait for you until June. Is that a deal?"

Robert smiled and kissed her again, "Deal." He had a thought, "Hold on. It's been a good day and I need to know whether I can do this." Robert stood up keeping Fran nestled in his arms.

"Robert!" she squealed, "Put me down. Your leg!"

"No Frannie. Let me try. I've been working out. I can leg press 400lbs, and my leg is getting stronger every day. What's the point of having two good legs, if I can't tuck my woman in?"

Fran held on and let Robert carry her where he would. He enjoyed the power in his actions. Fran felt lighter in his arms than the 250lbs he was up to on the bench press, and much more accommodating snuggled against his chest. He focused on moving with grace as he navigated the lamp at the living room door and made it down the hall.

At the foot of the stairs, he said, "So far, so good. You up for me trying to get you up the twenty risers to your second floor?"

"Sure. I'm praying that both of us won't break our necks, but I'm willing to hold still and let you try."

"Fran, you're a fun girl, that Norman better come back here and snap you up. You'd be a riot all the time and you are a lot of fun to cuddle."

Robert made it up all the stairs and down the hall into Fran's master bedroom. With a small shudder, he deposited her on the bedspread and crouched over her for a second.

Concerned, Fran sat up and asked, "Oh Robert. Was it too much? Are you okay?"

He shook his head And after a moment said, "Actually that went better than I thought. Carrying a snuggly girl is a heck of a lot easier than iron bars; the thigh is just spasming. I need to hold still for a minute to see if it calms down."

Fran lay back resting on her elbows, content to wait. "Ok. Fine with me, I like the view from here."

Robert laughed, "See, Frannie, you are funny as

hell. Here I am crouched over you, possibly stuck forever and you make a sexy pose, and sit there looking at me making wisecracks." Robert's spasm ended all of a sudden and he stood straight. He flexed his body, checking for trouble spots, but everything seemed ok. He rubbed his thigh where the spasm had hit and massaged for a minute. "All good. I call that a success. Thanks for letting me experiment on you, Fran."

"Anytime Robert. You do know that was a first time for me too."

Robert looked shocked, "You're kidding, no guy has ever carried you off?"

She smiled, "Nope. I wonder whether anyone other than a big, bad ex-FBI agent would dare. I've seen Mitch throw Jenny over his shoulder a couple of times, but none of the men I know man-handle their women. I also thought I was too big."

Robert sighed, "Fran, none of that. You are not fat, and if you are a bit tall, I am taller, bigger, and a heck a lot tougher. If anything makes you too much it's that smart mouth." Robert emphasized his feelings by leaning over her and kissing her senseless again. "I'm sorry the guys out here in Utah are too girlie to show you how much fun it is to play caveman. If Norm abandons you, on our way back here from the temple, I'll carry you in over the threshold, down your hellish long hall, and all the way up here. That's a promise."

***

The next week, the mason delivered the mantle and Robert finished the front chimney and fireplace surround.

Fran had an appointment with a prospective client the day Robert placed the last brick, so he wasn't sure he should wait to tell her goodbye in person. Robert went back and forth trying to decide whether to wait for Fran or just take off as he cleaned up the trappings of his masonry. In the week since he'd realized he'd be happy to be Fran's man, he'd tried to honor their agreement, but he was pretty sure he'd never let her go to Norm at Christmas if he stayed much longer. And in the back of his mind, he thought about Reva. He needed to figure stuff out before he did anything irrevocable with either Fran or Reva. Finally, he made his decision. He could be man enough to leave, but he didn't think he had the courage to tell Fran goodbye to her face. So, he cleaned up, packed his gear and Sam, and left a note for Fran on the mantle.

"Time to finally go home to Grand Junction," Robert said to Sam as he locked the front door from the outside. He dropped his key through her mail slot and headed to the loaded Jeep. On his way down to get on I-15 to get to I-70, he considered stopping to tell Mitch and Jenny goodbye, but decided against it. *If I stop before I get there, I will never go back and face the family. It's now or never, and if I hurry I can get home by Thanksgiving.*

***

Tears ran down her face as Fran read Robert's note.

'Because we are both are now healed, it would be a shame to hurt those we love by falling into something new before we have resolved our open issues. I could really love you, Frannie, but I am not sure I should. If it's meant to be, I'll come back to you. I would be honored to be your man. Love, Robert'.

When she'd gotten home, Fran had seen that his Jeep was gone, but she'd automatically assumed he was out doing errands, not gone for good. She looked back towards the front door and saw Robert's house key lying there on the floor. She'd walked right over it on her way in.

Chapter Twenty-Eight
Grandpappy's Cabin

Sam stood with his paws on the dash of the open-topped Jeep. Robert's grandpa had kept this old army Jeep up on the high ground for general use around the old homestead. Usually, it lived in the barn and looked like it. Robert had swiped a thick layer of dirt off the windshield and decided it was a worthless task without water, and laid the windshield down on the hood. Evidently Sam preferred this method of transit. He could stand high and didn't have to look sideways out the passenger window to smell the outside like he did in Robert's Cherokee. Robert shivered, thankful for his heavy coat, gloves and hat. December in Colorado was not conducive to driving around in such a vehicle.

"I'm glad Grandma didn't let this place go to hell when Grandpappy died. It's good that I'm her favorite grandson, too. I doubt she'd let anyone else up here."

Robert finally felt settled. Nearly four years out and he could almost function. Today was his 'there's a break in the weather' trip for gas. He'd maybe grab some grocery staples too. His grandmother, or mother, would do all his other shopping except groceries. Through some feminine conspiracy they determined that even single men with fear of civilization would have to find some way to feed themselves. Grandma had even stopped doing his laundry, and had paid to repair the old homestead's cabin back door, so he could add a washer and dryer. Robert had tried to stop her with an argument about how the rural septic system couldn't possibly handle more plumbing.

His grandmother responded stating, "Shut your trap. Your grandpappy put in extensive septic lines when we installed indoor plumbing in that cabin 40 years ago. The well can handle it too. He always meant to put a washer and dryer up there for me, but we never got around to it, because we'd come down each weekend for church and just did our laundry Saturday night. Besides, you know how he always planned to expand the cabin—when he last had the equipment up there, he dug the holes for his future cabin, not the 100-year-old structure that remains."

He'd made peace with his family and while things were still tense with his mother and sister, his grandmother, dad, and brother welcomed him back with open arms.

Robert shuddered to remember that first visit. He'd made it to his grandma's from Fran's in one day. His grandma was waiting; he'd called to give her a heads up at lunch. He was so happy to see her again, and she seemed glad to have him back. She immediately took to Sam, too, and she seemed ecstatic to move Robert and Sam into her spare bedroom.

Robert had spent the afternoon going through the mail his grandmother had stored for him and chatting with her. Robert enjoyed how his grandma had handled his mail. When Amanda first threatened divorce, he'd immediately separated all their finances and changed his mailing address to his grandma's house in Grand Junction. Through the years since, his grandma faithfully took care of his mail. She'd shredded all the junk mail and called Robert when something big came in. As for the rest, she just stored it. Robert kept track of his banking, credit cards, and bills online, so his grandmother only received his annual statements if anything. His accountant and lawyer would email critical items to him, but mailed the hard copies of everything to his grandma. She had one box just for legal things, which included the divorce papers, his tax returns, and the property documents from the Dallas house. She'd then bundled the rest of his mail by type and then by year and month.

Robert had also asked his mom and sister to store all his DC stuff they packed at Grandma's. Because his grandmother had worried about his stuff, she'd taken that first summer he was in the hospital and gone through it all. She trashed what she considered junk, stored what was worth saving and then jettisoned everything but his clothes, music, and books.

Robert thought about his remaining stuff and tried to figure how many trips between the homestead and Grand Junction it would take to get it up here. He pictured the spare room as it was and tried to mentally calculate the square footage of his Cherokee with the back seats removed. Grandma had turned her spare room into his. The dresser and closet held his clothes. The bookshelf held his books. File boxes stored his other stuff, and the rest of the wall space was filled with shelves of music—his albums and CDs. His mom *had* kept his music, and Grandma has displayed it with pride. Robert decided standing there in the room his grandma built for him, that he'd inherited any organizational skills he had from her. He'd laughed out loud when he'd realized his Grandma had *alphabetized* his music by artist.

During his first night in Grand Junction, Robert's parents came over for dinner. Grandma facilitated the discussion that got loud, heated, and mean before it calmed down. She then ran interference between Robert and his brother and sister on the following Sunday, when the whole family converged on her place for dinner after church. Robert had cringed when his siblings had begun to lay into him, but Grandma was right there,

"Knock it off, you two. If you cannot speak respectfully in this house, you can leave. Also, whatever problems you have with Robert are probably not his fault, so think long and hard before you rail at him again."

His brother said, "We'll talk later."

Grandma cut him off, "You will not. I know what's bugging you, and it's not his fault, so get over yourself, James." Grandma then turned to Kelly, "You've been talking to your mom, but I think you need to talk to your dad before you talk to Robert gain." That ended the meal on a more peaceful, if tense, note.

Since then, Robert made a trip into Grand Junction each week, usually on Saturday. He'd get his provisions and load Grandma's fridge with them as temporary storage, then he'd spend the night and go to church with her in the morning. They'd eat dinner with whichever family members showed up. On later Sundays, Robert began reforming a relationship with his siblings and parents. He made great in-roads by getting reacquainted with his nieces and nephews, and now his siblings and cousins, included him in their adult-conversation groups when everybody got together.

Robert was glad that his extended family had made room for him in their midst. He was surprised to learn he wasn't the only divorcee, nor the only out-of-work guy in the clan.

As they reached Parachute, Colorado, Robert remarked to Sam "This is so much better than staying in Jonesey's cabin. This is my grandpappy's place and I can make it mine."

He and Sam often stood in the front room of the cabin looking out the large window at the scenic vista of the mountain's valley. Here in the old homestead halfway between Parachute and Grand Junction, Colorado, the land perched on the edge of a mountain overlooking the mighty Colorado River far below.

In Parachute, Robert was glad the gas station's car wash was open today. *Probably so folks can wash off the road salt*, he thought. He pulled the old jeep into the wash bay and hosed off the worst of the dirt. Losing years of grime improved things, and he used an old chamois to clean both sides of the windshield, so he and Sam could have a windbreak on the way home. Robert then motored down to the gas pumps to fill up the Jeep and the three twenty-gallon auxiliary gas tanks he'd brought with him.

The spare gas helped him keep the generators going when the storms cut the power. He'd fill up the Cherokee on his next run.

As he swiped his debit card at the pump, Robert considered his money situation. Thankfully, Stan had banked all of his pay during his long recuperation, and the disability payments started after that. "I am pretty sure Jonesey didn't take a penny for all the help he gave me, and I know Mitch and Jenny didn't. That reminds me, maybe I can go back to carving bowls to make money. I'll have to ask Amy about that." He remarked to Sam as he pumped gas.

He frowned when his thoughts turned to Fran. *She certainly didn't need my money, nor did she want it.* Thinking of Fran led to thoughts of Reva, and Robert was still confused over those feelings. *I need to figure out who I want and let the other go.*

Gas tanks filled, Robert stopped at the small grocers' on the way home. He picked up milk, eggs, and flour to augment his staples at home. For the hundredth time, he was grateful that Jenny and Sam had cured his grocery store phobia. It helped that this grocer was the same as it had been when he'd been here with his grandpa as a kid and it felt 'safe'. He'd only been in Colorado for a few weeks, but it already felt like home, even on these rare sunny days in the middle of winter.

Chapter Twenty-Nine
Reva Leaves DC

Reva stood in the middle of her storage unit and surveyed her progress. Instead of heading to Colorado that day she'd left Jenny's she'd come home to DC and had a long talk with Stan. It seemed he finally understood that she wasn't sure what she wanted to do. He'd agreed to let her finish her time off without any more phone calls from him.

Gratefully, Reva had rented an apartment in DC for a month, so she could deal with the stuff from her condo. She'd worked out a tentative plan: She'd go through all her stuff and whittle it down to what she'd 'have to move' when she found a new home. Then she'd jettison the rest and keep what remained in storage for now. After all that she'd decide about her car. She could pay to transport it somewhere or she could just drive it there. She didn't want to sell it, but was keeping that as an option of last resort.

From where she stood, Reva could see that she'd only partially filled the rented medium moving van, she had succeeded in taking her stuff down to the minimum level. She now had room to store the Chevelle here with her remaining stuff in case she decided to leave it here. "For now, it's fine at the apartment's garage. Let's take this load to goodwill."

At the goodwill drop off point, Reva was glad to see the odds and ends of her family's furniture leave her hands. Over the two years between her brother moving to Tel Aviv and her Mother, Father, and Grandmother deciding to follow, she'd been the recipient of everything that one of the Findsteins couldn't ship to Israel, but didn't feel that they could throw away or donate. It had added up, and Reva was glad to be free of the load.

Reva then motored to the truck rental office. While waiting for the rental company to finalize the paper work to return the now-empty moving van, she fingered the phone number burning a hole in her pocket. She had told Stan about her plan to do some recon on Robert's family and he'd loved the idea. As his second in command, he'd given her Robert's parent's names, so she could investigate Robert's home situation, but he'd also included a phone number for Robert's grandmother. Robert had listed his grandmother as his 'out of state' emergency contact on his FBI paperwork. Stan thought, and Reva agreed that it meant that Robert got along with his grandmother better than his parents. She was the place to start.

When Reva got home she sat down to plan. Her stuff was stored. She had a week left on her lease, and what stuff she had left in this apartment would just fill the Chevelle's trunk. That decided her. She called the number in her pocket.

Robert's grandmother, Jeannie was a sweetheart. Reva had enjoyed their hour-long conversation and she thought Jeannie had too. Reva learned that Jeannie knew all about Robert's FBI career and had talked to Grant as well as Stan. *She also knew who I was... "the nice girl Stan wanted to be partners with my Robert."* That gave Reva some hope, so she'd pushed through with her request. Jeannie was excited and the two had plotted and combined plans with a single goal, to help Robert be happy.

Reva's plan was simple. She was going to drive to Grand Junction in her Chevelle and hang out there with Robert's grandmother until she knew one way or another how Robert felt about her. Reva smiled at herself. *I must be half in love with him already, or I would have freaked at his grandma's overt matchmaking. I don't mind being a wife-candidate for Robert. Not at all.*

Reva finished her packing and ran through the apartment a few times looking for stray items. Then she packed the fridge into her cooler. She planned to hotel when and where she felt like it, and if she had mini-fridges along the way; she could save money on food. She still had a nice nest egg from her condo sale, but she may need that for a new house when she settled, so she'd try to live conservatively for now.

An excited Reva drove out of DC in her Chevelle for its longest road trip, ever. She planned to aim for Denver and then cut south, but maybe she'd aim for Salt Lake and go that way to see Jenny on the way. She'd love to see Jenny's new babies. *Imagine. Twin girls at forty. WOW!* Maybe she should take up their offer to take their truck. She sure didn't want drive her Chevelle off-road. Reva thought of what Grandma Jeannie had said about Robert, "He's taken over my husband's family's old pioneer homestead, which is way off the beaten track."

Chapter Thirty
Reva Buys a Truck

"I am so glad Jenny gave me her old truck and let me use it to trade in on a new truck." Reva said to herself, as she cruised down I-70 south of Salt Lake City. Her new truck drove like a dream.

Reva had taken four days to get from DC to Ogden. Her Chevelle functioned perfectly and she was glad she'd kept it. At the Harpers, she spent a few days with Mitch and Jenny and the new babies. The girls were identical and were a mix of Jenny and Mitch with his dark hair, but Jenny's light eyes. Mitch and Jenny were glad to give Reva their old truck. They had bought a new truck, and had a 2009 Honda Odyssey, but were looking to get into an old Suburban that could hold the eight of them. They needed TRUCKY's parking spot for it.

Mitch had taken her and TRUCKY to the local GMC dealer. Reva had wondered whether his big, masculine presence would help with the salesman or not. Mitch ended up just walking with her saying nothing—For once, Reva got a female saleslady who was as car crazy as herself. Reva wondered what Mitch thought about their group as the three of them wandered the lot looking at new trucks, while the sales lady focused on showing Reva all the possible options. Reva ended up finding a slightly used 2013 GMC Sierra a lot like Mitch and Jenny's new truck. Unlike Mitch and Jenny, she didn't need the crew cab, so she picked her Sierra because it had all the goodies, a heavy towing package, an extended cab, and was a sparkly dark blue color.

Reva used some of her precious nest egg to buy the truck with cash. The cash price cut down the cost and the dealer gave her $1,500 in trade for Jenny's truck with its shell. Mitch was happy to sign over the title, then he and Reva walked out with the saleslady to transfer Reva's gear from TRUCKY to the new truck. The saleslady just watched and laughed as Reva and Mitch took off TRUKY's receiver hitch and put it in the new truck's hitch slot. Mitch opened TRUCKY's shell, and hefted the heavy rubber mat out of the bed. Because both trucks were extended cabs, they had similar beds and the mat fit just fine in the back of Reva's new truck. Reva figured she'd get a protective spray-in bed liner at some point in the future, but the rubber mat would gap her until then.

Mitch then rode with Reva to buy a used car-hauler trailer for her Chevelle from a guy he knew. Then as Jenny watched from the front room window, Mitch and Reva unpacked the Chevelle, moved the stuff into the new truck and bed, tarped the load, and then Mitch helped Reva drive her baby on its new trailer by spotting for her as she gingerly drove it up the ramp between the side rails. She was now fully stocked with her gear and fully mobile. Reva hugged Jenny, Mitch, their kids and the babies and headed where she needed to go—"Colorado and Robert, here I come."

Chapter Thirty-One
Thinking of Fran

Driving to Denver via I-70 and Grand Junction, CO from Ogden, UT felt silly. Reva hoped her reasons for going that way, and adding miles to her trip just to see Robert, was the right thing to do. She could just go to Denver via I-84 and I-80 like everyone else and stay safe with Jonesey's Denver Bunch. Reva was glad Jenny supported her plan—especially the part about involving Robert's grandma. *Jenny is right; I am fixated on Robert. The problem is what to do about it.*

Reva was always honest with herself. She couldn't delude herself about something even when she wanted to. She knew that she was obsessed with Robert, but she didn't want to admit it and she didn't know what to do about her Robert problem. This time, she didn't want to analyze why she felt the way she did or mull over why she was mooning over such an unattainable guy. *Oh well, you are stuck for now. You promised to present yourself to Jeannie for inspection.* Jeannie was sure she'd be a good fit and Reva felt she had an ally. *Maybe Jenny was right when she said, "Go get him!"*

Reva often wondered about Robert and Fran. She knew Fran from her periodic visits out to see Jenny over the years. Jenny had told her that Fran had helped Robert regain his confidence, and that Fran described Robert's progress as "he's achieved a feeling of inner peace, and could function in the real world." Reva thought about that then she imagined how Robert would feel about Fran. *Fran is gorgeous, and if she and Robert had shared a house for a while...* Reva cut off the thought. She had no right to be jealous, so she tried to focus on Robert's progress instead.

Reva thought about Robert's taking over the family homestead in the mountains. *How can living in an isolated cabin twenty miles from the nearest gas station on the edge of a national forest equate to living in 'the real world'?*

Of course, Jenny agreed with Fran. Robert could buy provisions, speak peaceably with strangers, and make it through a week with only one or two flashbacks. Fran had also taken Robert with her to church. Reva wasn't sure this was a sign of progress or not. For Jenny, the fact that he started going back to church meant he was cured. Reva didn't know how going to church could make someone cured. It made no sense to her. God to Reva was part of life, part of who she was. She'd recognized that Robert believed in God and prayed often. He just hadn't set foot in a church for fifteen years before now. Jenny had tried to explain it to her, but Reva remained skeptical. What was so special about the Mormon Church that a person attending services each Sabbath meant they were cured—that they were all right with their world?

Reva went to temple when the spirit moved her, not because of guilt or habit, but when she needed the recharge and companionship of others. Weekly devotions seemed rote to her. Having a relationship with God and being good was a way of life; something Reva did every day and all the time. Stepping into a building weekly to express obedience to God's commandments to keep the Sabbath holy seemed too much like the strict rules laid out in the Old Testament. Reva felt heretical, but she equated Jenny and Robert's weekly attendance in church to her own family's periodic, habitual pilgrimages to Jerusalem and the West Wall. Reva agreed that it was a holy place, but she believed that you could find God anywhere—you didn't need a building.

Her thoughts took Reva back to the genealogy discussion she'd had with Fran. Fran was now over fifty, and had never been married. She was the only single grandchild in Jenny's large extended family. Fran was a paradox to Jenny's Johnson clan. To them women were supposed to get married and have children. Other activities like a career or hobbies, or even art, followed after those things. Fran had started college as an art major, but switched to engineering and had been a career woman ever since. That she'd never married made sense to Reva, because she too had never 'found the right man.' Jenny's cousins thought that Fran had passed up on marriage because she was too focused on her career, and some looked down on her for it. Reva wondered what they would say about Fran's situation if they thought in terms of her past cancer.

On this trip, Reva had worried that Jenny's family would look on her in the same way. Reva too, had focused on her career and never married, and was now forty with no children or husband. These thoughts had been with her ever since she'd left Tel Aviv. She just wasn't sure that she wanted to be alone anymore, and her loneliness had motivated her to ask Stan for a leave of absence and sell her condo. *Would Jenny's family judge me as wanting because home and family is not and has not been my life?*

Jenny was upset when she heard about Reva's concern. Only some of her cousins, who were young and didn't know any better, had judged Fran. They didn't understand; nobody talked about Fran's cancer anymore, so it was possible that these younger cousins didn't know the story.

Fran always said that she'd never met someone she could give her heart to, and she wasn't worried about it. She had a life that fulfilled her and she was fine with her place in the world. Jenny had driven Reva over to see Fran and see the huge Victorian she was nearly through renovating. Reva had always liked Fran and worked to stop the jealousy that consumed her immediately when she'd learned that Robert had stayed there in that lovely old house with her. She'd focused on the brick work he'd done on the huge chimney in the front room instead. Somehow Reva had made it through the tour, and she tried hard to think of Fran objectively and not as a rival. Jenny had also told her to think about Fran's ex, Norm. *The two of them have dated on and off for the past few years, but Jenny thinks they are finished now.*

Norm or not, Fran had no problems enjoying her huge houses. She loved sharing her latest one with her dozens of nieces and nephews. She was the fun sister, the neat aunt, the one who had a smile for everyone; she just didn't have children of her own.

On her last night in Ogden, Reva had eaten dinner at Fran's house at her invitation.

Fran said, "Thank you for coming. Robert told me about you and I wanted to see how you were and get to know you better."

They had sat, two well-adjusted women eating a home-prepared dinner on fine china at Fran's antique dining table that sat twelve.

"This is the life God gave me." Fran said. "He didn't put a husband or children in my path, but I am okay with that. When I get feeling down, He lets me know I am okay and tells me to 'Count my Blessings' and I feel better."

Reva could tell Fran really was okay. She was comfortable in her own skin and didn't care what anyone else thought. Reva chose not to think that maybe Fran was sizing her up, comparing her as a rival for Robert's affection. *That's just serious jealousy. Jenny would have told you if Fran and Robert had had something brewing, so knock it off.*

However, the meal went well and, as they both relaxed, it was Fran who most eloquently explained her situation with the family. "I know I threaten them somehow. They could be envious about my freedom, or money, or the excitement of my job, but on the other hand, they see me as a 'dead end'. My line ends with me. Jenny and my mother are the genealogists in the family. Mom keeps all the records, including the family group sheets where we show the married couples with their kids with their birth and death dates. My sheet is still empty. My line ends here, with me. That's an unsettling thought for a genealogist...the end of a line. It makes some, including me sometimes, uncomfortable. Our church says 'families are forever' and we believe in the covenant given to Abraham, but I will have no issue, no heirs, so where do I fit in God's kingdom?"

At that point, Fran had looked away and was quiet for a moment before answering her own question. "That's not the point really. I am responsible for me and my life. So, while I don't have children now, I will in the future. If I live my life to my potential, God will judge me worthy and I will have a family in the next life." Fran had then explained that there would be a spot in her family for her, and she wasn't the only 'maiden aunt' in the many branches. "At the least, when I die, all those other unattached sisters are going to grab me and we're gonna have a heck of a hen party." Fran quipped.

Reva thought about Fran and prayed for forgiveness for her mean thoughts towards her. *Heck, if Fran is the right woman for Robert, I wish them both the best. At least Fran will really love him and move heaven and earth to keep him happy. She's a classy lady. I doubt I could have been nice to the rival for the man I loved.*

Chapter Thirty-Two
A Sunday Morning in Grand Junction

Robert yanked on his tie to loosen it from his throat. He was running a little late and wondered for the hundredth time why he hadn't come down to Grandma's last night. Now, here he was speeding down the road on a Sunday morning so he could get Grandma to church on time. As he pulled in her long drive, he saw a strange blue truck parked by her garage. A car trailer was hitched to the back of the truck holding what looked like a cherry-red classic Chevy Chevelle. As he got closer, he saw a Utah plate on the trailer and a temporary Utah sticker on the truck's back window.

"Who the heck does Grandma know from Utah? Could that be Reva's Chevelle? It's not Mitch's truck, Jenny made him get a green crew cab." Then he spotted the Maryland plates on the Chevelle.

Robert's palms began to sweat and a warm feeling came over him. He didn't put a voice to his thoughts, but he knew Reva could have come through Utah to see Mitch and Jenny. *Could she have bought a truck just to drive her Chevelle down here?* Trying to stay calm, Robert parked the Jeep and shrugged into his suit coat. "Come on, Sam." He took two steps towards his Grandma's front door, when it opened. "Oh my God, that's Reva!" Robert spoke aloud, shocked to his core.

Reva came through the door sideways helping his grandma step over the threshold. She then let Grandma go first to him. Robert stood staring at Reva trying to believe that she was real, that she was really here in Grand Junction, in his home. His grandma reached him and then tugged on his tie to get his attention, "Make it quick, Robbie, we're late for church." Robert looked down to her and said absently, "'K, Grandma. I'll try."

Robert moved past his grandmother and met Reva

on the porch. He couldn't believe what he was seeing. Here she was, in the flesh. Heedless of Sam and Grandma watching, Robert paused on the top step as he stared at Reva face to face.

She said, "Robert?"

He moved forward and grabbed her, holding her tightly in his arms. Reva grabbed him back reflexively and then held on just as hard. Robert just held her with one arm for a while as he made soft strokes down her hair with his left hand. He kept stroking to her shoulder and then back up. He buried his face against the right side of her head and neck, saying over and over,

"Oh, God Reva, you're here. You're real. You're really here. I can't believe it."

***

Reva couldn't help the tears of joy that spilled from her eyes. Happiness filled her. She was in the right place at last. She couldn't believe she was really here with Robert: that she was in his arms, that he had apparently missed her as much as she'd missed him. She and Grandma Jeannie had plotted a whole scenario to get Robert to admit he cared for her. Reva had spent all night thinking of what she would say and how she would say it, but words failed her— thankfully they weren't needed. She gave up the words and relished the feel of Robert in her arms, the feel of his flesh beneath the cloth under her fingers. She clutched at his back and leaned into him for as much as she was worth.

***

Robert was so happy, his eyes were leaking. He quit talking and moved his hands to frame Reva's face. He pulled her long curls away from her mouth with his thumb and then leaned in and kissed her to tell her without words how he felt about her. In that moment he absolutely knew that while he could be Fran's man, that that was not his primary purpose. He *knew* that he'd been put on this earth in this moment to be here with Reva. Reva was his life. She was his light, and he could do nothing but be her man for now and forever. In that moment God answered his prayer and let him know unequivocally that this was right and Reva was the one for him.

Robert realized that Reva was squeezing him tightly and silently crying at the same time. He became conscious that Sam was trying to nose in between them, but couldn't because they were clutching each other too tightly. He decided he didn't care to placate the dog at the same time he decided his leg was killing him. He swung Reva up into his arms, turned and headed into the house, kicking the door closed on Sam, and headed to his bedroom.

Robert's single thought was to get Reva to his bedroom and his bed. He made it two steps into the house, when his Grandma's voice stopped him cold, "Robert Leland, just what are you doing? For heaven's sake, it's the Sabbath. Put her down!"

He stopped there in the living room and let Reva down, but he didn't let go of her. Embarrassment and male dominance fought in his brain.

Reva started giggling.

Robert wouldn't let her pull away, so he turned them towards Grandma at the door. "Sorry, Grandma. It's just that I haven't seen Reva for months and I never got the chance last August to tell her I love her. I need a moment with her."

Grandma looked him in the eye and looked at Reva, who chimed in,

"Jeannie, this is my fault. I ran out on him, and we never got to have the heart-to-heart talk that we needed."

Robert felt Reva shrug.

Grandma looked to heaven and then turned back and opened the door, "Get in here, Sam. We're not going anywhere." She turned back to them and held out her hand, "Rob, give me your phone so I can text your dad to tell him we won't be to church today."

Robert let go of Reva long enough to fish his cell phone out of his suit pocket. Grandma walked past them to the kitchen and Sam followed her.

Reva looked up at him, and asked, "Were you carrying me off to the nearest bed, in front of Grandma Jeannie and on your Sabbath?"

Robert hid his face in her neck and confessed, "I was. I totally was. If Grandma hadn't have stopped me, we'd be there now. I am so sorry."

Reva smiled, "Well I am not sorry, but maybe you're right. There is an order to things and there are better times and places to get closer."

He laughed and then nuzzled her neck. Reva started to wiggle and playfully tried to get away. Robert lifted his head, "Hold still, I need my snuggle time before you tell me why the hell you came here, to Colorado."

Grandma came back into the room. "Break it up, you two. What's the plan?"

Robert looked down to Reva who shrugged. He spoke, "I'm not sure. I got caught up in the moment. What's your plan, Reva?"

Reva smirked, "My plan was to work with your grandma to get you to admit that you liked me. So, plan worked from what I can tell."

Robert laughed, "Better than expected, I'd say." He turned back to Grandma, "Reva and I have some talking we need to do and some things to figure out. Can you keep Sam here for a time while I take Reva for a ride?"

"When will you be back?"

Robert looked down to Reva, "Probably by bed time. Don't hold dinner for us." With that he released Reva, gave his grandmother a hug, and then pulled Reva out of the house to his Jeep.

As he handed her up into the seat, he voiced a thought that just hit him, "Are you okay going in my Jeep or do you want to take your new truck?"

Reva laughed, "Your Jeep is fine. I don't feel like unhitching my Chevelle right now." Robert pulled out of his Grandma's and headed back to the homestead. He needed Reva to see it, to know if it would work for her, for them. They could work out everything else later. He needed to find out if his woman could live in his house, or if he needed to find another one.

Chapter Thirty-Three
Reva and Robert

"I've been there, you know. You aren't the only one who has stood on the edge and looked down and weren't scared—just deciding how to jump." Reva spoke.

Robert looked at her. Others had tried to convince him that he wasn't alone in an effort to bring him back into the fold, the FBI fold.

Remarks like: "That's too bad." "He was such a fine agent." "It just gets to some." were the most typical sentiments he'd heard or overheard. "So your partner died, get over it." "It's unfortunate that you were tortured; move on."

He could never fit how he felt into those statements. All the counselors, all the doctors, all those 'psychos' didn't get it. They couldn't. They hadn't been there, but Reva had.

Meanwhile, Reva was still talking. Robert observed her. Ever since he'd come out west, his FBI buddies had gone out of their way to put their women into his face. They seemed to collectively figure that if their woman helped them during trials, that she'd be able to help him. He appreciated all of them. He liked Jonesey's wife Amy's cooking. He thought Jenny, Mitch's wife, was the best looking second only to Reva, herself, with those legs and all that hair. But, Reva was different. He hadn't placed her yet. He couldn't really categorize her. Looking over at her, he decided that maybe he didn't need to; she was just Reva, just his gorgeous, wonderful woman.

"It's no wonder that the veterans are coming home scarred and can't be fixed. We don't seem to have the tools to deal with their new reality in our make-believe world." Reva just said.

Robert let it pass over him. He agreed with her, but didn't say so. Despite its official name, he preferred the term 'shell-shocked.' It gave him a much better picture of Post-Traumatic-Stress-Disorder. Like all the other 'ailments' of this American culture, this disorder had made it into the everyday. He felt better when this label was slapped on him when he thought of farm boys coming home from the trenches and dreaming of yellow gas, shells, mud, and faces in gas masks amongst tall corn, starry nights, and the quiet of a pre-media time.

The FBI agents' 'wives' he'd met worried about his looks, his weight, his cleanliness, and his hair. They seemed to think that a good meal, shower, and haircut would fix the shadows in his eyes. Amy was the easiest to be around. It wasn't her food or her house; it was her quiet. She had the most peaceful way about her. He knew that's how Jonesey stayed sane. Amy also had the best smells in her house. Natural things like herbs, but she also had those smelly candles here and there. She'd given him a tin box he could open when he wanted the smell. A friend sold candles and warmers from her home. She'd sold this box to Amy and called it a 'travel kit.' Robert didn't know the name of the flavor, but Amy did, and she'd mail him new boxes every few weeks. He liked it mostly, because it smelled nothing like the back end of a busy grocery store.

The worst smell was blood, but smelling strawberries, especially rotting ones, got Robert every time. He knew Reva got the smell thing too. He was glad that his woman could help him with the worst side effect of his torture. He would always remember the herbs she'd packed to soothe and calm his leg.

Thank God, that Mitch understood the smell thing. He and Robert had been driving in Ogden one day and they'd passed the dog-food factory. Robert had turned white when the smell came through the car vents. Mitch asked what, but Robert couldn't talk.

"Hey, man, is it the dog food?"

Robert could nod, barely. Mitch sped up and pulled

over once they passed the smell zone. Robert tried the counting thing Jenny did. 1000, 999, 998, 997… Jenny told him to breathe for each number and focus on not missing any. He knew that the breaths would help get oxygen in his body and get the adrenalin moving on, but he still hated any 'relaxation exercises.' Because the smell wasn't so bad a mile past the factory, he recovered quickly. By the time he'd counted down to 950 he was able to talk. Mitch had never worked in a grocery store, so he'd been surprised at what smells permeated the stock area, but accepted that dry dog food was a reasonable smell found there.

Mitch had only understood Robert's reaction when he'd learned that one of the Renata brothers had accidently knocked over a torn 50lb bag of dog food, and the pellets surrounded he and Alan during the torture. Like the smell of strawberries and rotten tomatoes, the grainy smell of most dog foods took Robert immediately to the back of that grocery.

Poor Sam, Robert had tried nearly fifty dog food brands before he'd found one that both he and Sam could live with. Sam hated canned food for some reason, and the cereal smell of most dry brands was too hard on Robert. That was the main reason Jenny and he had begun making homemade dog food.

Reva got the smell thing. She knew it. That was one thing Robert was learning about her. She *had* been there. She knew. He wasn't sure all of her details, but she had been dealing with her issues for a decade from what Stan had said. Reva had even been back to that pub in London where Carl had died. She hadn't said much, only that her arm hurt. Robert wondered how she'd really describe it. Some things don't work well with words. Ache, throbbed, vibrated painfully, that's how he'd bet she'd describe how her healed broken arm, or the year-old gunshot wound, had felt.

Robert stood up to stretch his leg. He and Reva had

sat and talked all afternoon. "Now that we've made sense of a lot of stuff, I need to show you around before I take you back to Grandma's."

Reva looked at him questioningly, "What's there to see? This is your home, your grandpa's cabin right?"

Robert smiled at her, "You told me once that you couldn't live off the grid, not even if you were living with me, so I need you to see how bad it is here so I know whether or not I have to go house hunting before you'll marry me."

Reva stood up and pressed her palm against his cheek, "I am so sorry for that damn note. I'll live where you live. I follow where you go. I came to Colorado didn't I? Besides your cabin is only a half-mile from the pavement. It's not Jonesey's cabin, which is 100 miles from the nearest highway. In four hours we could be in downtown Denver."

Robert toured Reva through the three levels in the cabin holding hands. She admired the warm tones of the pine paneling and the hardwood floors. He could tell she loved the quilt Grandma had made for his bed, and she sighed over the view down to the Colorado River from the front room.

She paused for a moment when he went to leave the window and asked, "Robert?"

"Yes."

"What color is the Colorado River?"

Robert was slightly surprised by her question but didn't show it, when he answered it, "Oh. Down there it turns green when the algae bloom. Why?"

"Oh, just wondered."

Robert moved to go into the next room saying, "I think you'll love it in the summer. There's a trail down to Grandpappy's eddy pool. We could go skinny dipping."

Reva didn't answer Robert or move with him, but clutched his arm instead.

Robert stopped and watched her face. He saw her go pale, "What is it? What's wrong? Are you ok?" He pulled her against her chest and felt her shudder.

Reva finally looked up, "Oh God, Robert, it's my dream. I've been dreaming of you and me in my river. It was green, and there's a dusty trail down to it, but I didn't know it was your river, that it was the Colorado, and just now, I saw an image of that eddy pool. I am sure your grandpa's pool is OUR pool, and that scares me."

Robert felt a confirmation from heaven come through his body in a warm feeling and words came pouring out of his mouth, "No Reva. Don't be scared. It was a true dream. It's our river. I love you and we're meant to be together. Your dream is proof. I've had it too."

***

They made it back to Grandma's in time for dinner. Neither was surprised to see Robert's parents and siblings and their children. Reva enjoyed being pulled into the Leland family.

After dinner she walked Sam and Robert out to the Jeep. He kissed her deeply before getting ready to go, "So Reva, do I court you from here?"

Reva paused then said, "I am not sure. I could certainly stay here with your Grandma, but I wondered if we'd offend everyone if I just stayed with you." Reva stopped when she saw Robert's eyes blaze, "No, not like that. I don't mean *live* with you, at least not yet. I mean be your roommate so I can get to know you better and you can get to know me, really, to see if we are really suited for each other. I can't be myself around your Grandma, and I think that my insomnia would pair well with your nightmares. Can we try that?"

Robert thought for a minute, "You're probably right. We're both still learning about each other. I think it can work, but if things get too hot, I'm bringing your butt back here until the wedding. I'm too old to risk my eternal salvation by jumping you before we're married. Now, if Grandma hadn't have stopped us earlier, there'd be no question of me holding back. However, she did stop me and now that the blood has made it back to my head, I have to agree you are right. There's more to love than sex. Let's try a two-week period. At the end of which, or earlier, you marry me and we live together as husband and wife."

"You've got a deal. I do love you, Robert. Be safe and come back tomorrow to get me and we'll start our two weeks tomorrow."

Chapter Thirty-Four
Roommates

Early Monday morning, Robert and Sam went to Grandma's to get Reva and her two-weeks' of gear for their trial run. Robert knew that he could live happily with Reva for the rest of his life, just by how easy she was to work with. She hauled heavy boxes without a murmur, and happily worked with him to stow her boxes, the trailer, and the Chevelle in Grandma's garage.

They went back to the homestead in a convoy with Reva following Robert's Jeep in her truck. Sam had followed her to her truck as if to say that he wanted to ride with her. Reva laughed and let him up on the passenger seat. "Robert, what happens if we get snowed in?"

"Then we wait until we can get out. I have provisions for up to a month. Put your coat in the back seat and let's go, woman."

It only took a few minutes to stow Reva's gear in the spare bedroom just down from Robert's master. She shyly, but efficiently placed her toothbrush and paste next to his in the medicine cabinet in the only bathroom upstairs. She then placed her soap and herbal hair concoctions on the shelf next to his shampoo in the shower.

Robert smiled as he watched her finger his soft towels hanging on the bar. "Are you okay using my towels?" He asked.

She blushed and nodded. Robert could just imagine what she was thinking. He hoped she was picturing him toweling off, because he could certainly imagine her wet from the shower in just a towel.

They then went downstairs into the multi-purpose room. Robert explained as they dropped off Reva's exercise gear, "Grandpappy dug down a basement access to the back pasture and the trail through it that sloped downhill to the river. Great-grandpa used this path to get to his animals in the pasture. I use the trail as a shortcut to the river on hot days." He explained to Reva, "In the 1950s, Grandpappy poured a new foundation down here and made a patio with the leftover cement. He also put in the glass doors to let in some light. Grandma made him leave room for a washer and dryer, though no one installed a set until I moved in. I've been working out here as you can tell from my weights."

Reva eyed the space and gestured with her hands measuring it in her mind, "Are you okay if I put some tumble mats down? I figure the span is about ten feet by twenty, right?"

Robert nodded.

"Good, that gives me room to do my maneuvers while still leaving you room for your weights."

Robert couldn't wait to see Reva in action. The DC office and Mitch sang her praises when speaking about her fighting skills, but he'd yet to see her in action. He pictured the mats she'd need, and mentally calculated the stuff he'd unpacked from her truck, "Hey, you didn't bring your mats with you, did you?"

"Oh no, I left what few I had in DC. I donated them to a local after school program. I was thinking we'd go to Denver tomorrow or the next day and get some more for here. I have a connection in Denver through Jonesey, when I set up the Denver Bunch's gym."

Robert impulsively hugged her, "Can I say that I find my woman talking about gym mats sexy?"

Reva laughed, and kissed him hard, "Well, I am getting them for you. I'll need a sparring partner, and I don't want to hurt your beautiful body any more than it's already been hurt." She maneuvered out of reach and swatted his butt before she lightly ran up the stairs.

Chapter Thirty-Five
Getting to Know You

"Why did you end up coming out west from DC; I mean besides me?" Robert asked Reva.

"Mostly because of Jonesey and Jenny," Reva responded. "When my brother took my parents and Grandma to Tel Aviv, I was the last one here in America. I thought about my grandpa and how much he loved America and I couldn't leave. But, I also couldn't stay in Baltimore. The memories there were too thick and there was no one I loved left there. So, I asked Stan for a leave of absence and put my condo up for sale as an experiment. To my surprise it sold in two weeks for more than my asking price, so I found myself with no home and time on my hands."

Reva leaned back into Robert as she went on, "I tried Tel Aviv for a while. Living with Mom and Dad and Grandma was like being a teenager again, and I really didn't get a chance to experience my own life with them. It was worse with my brother; he's living a high-class banker lifestyle just like he did in Boston and D.C., but in a Jewish way as he's now operating out of Tel Aviv. His way ain't my way, and never has been. When I came back to the states, I had a long chat with Stan…"

Robert interrupted Reva, "One of his coffee talks that takes hours, huh."

"Yes. He told me he was curious about Israel, but really, he was just taking my 'mental temperature.' It was that talk that convinced me I was done. I had taken a six-month leave of absence and was consulting on a couple of cases, but my heart was no longer in it."

Reva unconsciously felt her shoulder where the Renatas had shot her. "It started after the gunshot. I felt like I was done with the FBI, but hadn't realized it. Stan did, though and asked me about my future. I knew I couldn't stay in DC anymore. If I couldn't be FBI, there was nothing there for me, no partner, no family, no friends. No life. Stan told me I could transfer to another office and offered me my choice. I didn't know how to decide so I called Jonesey and Mitch. I figured Mitch had chosen Salt Lake due to Jenny, which he confirmed. I knew Jonesey chose Boise because of his wilderness, and that's true, but he told me his roots are in those mountains...they were in his blood. He said that he could have worked anywhere, but when the job got to be too much, he needed his wilderness and mountains to maintain sanity. He's the one who told me to pick a new home based on the place. He said if I could find a place that spoke to me, I could grow new roots, find new friends and make my own new family. Of course, I put Denver high on the list, because of you." She smiled and leaned back to give him a long, savored kiss.

***

Robert thought about what Reva had said and his own experiences. They sat in the early morning by the first fire of the day, him drinking cocoa and Reva her strong coffee. Robert knew he had come back to Colorado to heal himself, his body, and his relationship with his family. Jonesey had recognized his problem, and offered him solace elsewhere, knowing that it would be hard for him to go home.

When that solitude had been insufficient, Mitch had stepped in and gave him mountains, freedom, and Jenny's family, which was the perfect mix to restart his life. Now that he was healed sufficiently, he thought of his latest conversation with Stan. Stan was okay to let him stay on disability, but equally willing to let him come back to work if Robert could find an office or post that suited his new life. Robert thought about how he'd enjoyed working in the DC office, but preferred the Dallas office's laidback style. He'd enjoyed living in Texas where he'd hated living in Virginia. He thought about how he hated the Denver agents' snobbery about the rest of Colorado and how Grand Junction had been infected with the California-ism of other Colorado towns like Vale and Aspen.

Could he go back to the FBI? He wasn't sure, and now he didn't think he'd like living anywhere else, but here. Now that he and Sam had got the cabin set up the way they liked it, it felt like home, even more so with Reva here. As Robert thought, he could understand where Jonesey was coming from. His roots were here. His family had come here, and though they'd come for a new life, for a job, and for a religion, they'd stayed here, because these mountain valleys had become home to them.

He looked at Reva and thought about her life. He spoke, "We two are a lot alike. We both have issues with our mothers. I also lost a grandfather who was everything to me. Both of us have siblings who understand some things, but are clueless about others. But, at least my brother and sister know me well enough to know when to back off. And, my Grandma is a fine mother to me when I need it."

Robert nuzzled his chin against the top of Reva's head savoring the smell and feel of her curly hair. "You don't have any family support left, do you? Your brother sounds clueless and I bet your mom wants to morph you into a Jewish princess and so you can help resettle the homeland."

Reva laughed, "You are SO right. I should tell you about the Jerusalem policeman Mom set me up with. He was *too* much for me—too intense. I felt like pretending to be a Palestinian princess just to push his buttons."

Robert smiled picturing the intensity of that guy. "I wish I could have seen that. I agree that Israel is a good thing. The Israelis deserve a homeland... But, folks should get to make their own decisions." He paused, "Did Jenny ever tell you about how the Mormons came out here? I think I'm a lot like my own forebears. My grandpa's family came west to Utah with the Mormons during the pioneer migration, but when Brigham Young had told my great-great-great grandfather to uproot his family and go to Mexico, my great-grandfather did it for just one winter, where he early died. He gave it up and returned north—all soured on the prophet and Mormonism.

"He was like Butch Cassidy. He took up cattle thieving along the Utah and Colorado border. He met a bad end, and left behind a young wife and two surviving daughters. Grandma always focuses on their story. She talks about how they rekindled their faith and went on. Grandma says my great-great-great-grandmother buried a baby in Mexico, another in Grand Junction, and then her husband. But, she never left the faith, and did what she could to stay Mormon even when her husband died, leaving her abandoned in Colorado on her own. She did what she could, married a local rancher, converted him to her religion, and the family stayed here in this valley living, dying and growing new generations ever since. Of course, we've tried to stay on the right side of the law since then."

Reva smiled, "Which is why you are a big bad FBI agent instead of a drug dealer, right?"

"You got it!"

"You Mormons must all have stories like that. Yours reminded me of Jenny's. She had a great-great grandfather who had bought a new farm, but was immediately called on a mission for the church. Rather than leave the farm and his family, he chose to stay and get the farm going. Instead it failed. She said her family ended up penniless and moved to the Browning Ranch in northern Utah for work. She'd always said that she tried to do what God told her to do, because doing otherwise carried a heavy penalty."

Robert agreed, "I have to agree with her there. I had a bad vibe about moving me and my ex to DC. I had prayed over the office choice, and God gave me a clear impression to go to Dallas, not DC, but I really wanted DC and I went there anyway. If I had gone to Dallas earlier, maybe we'd not be having this conversation."

Robert shifted feeling uncomfortable with the subject, but continued, "I can see now, that DC politics helped turned my ex into a social climbing, trophy wife. By the time we finally moved to Dallas, my marriage was already in deep trouble. Maybe we'd still be together and have a passel of kids like Mitch and Jenny if we'd gone to Dallas first." Robert squeezed Reva's shoulders to ease the sting of having her hear about his ex, "Of course, I would do it all again to have you instead. You're a million times the woman my ex will ever be. I love you, baby."

They kissed.

Reva started talking again, "Jonesey told me to pick Denver or Vegas if I liked it out here. He says that these two offices are big enough, but western enough to suit me. He said to avoid Phoenix because I'd spend all my time with immigration and drug cartel cases. He said California was crazy and I'd have to pick a region and stick to it, but that I'd hate the sprawl of LA.

"He also said the potheads and homeless in Portland and Seattle might be fun for me. He hates dealing with the free spirits up there, but that I may like it. I like San Diego, but it's too hot. I liked Seattle over Portland, but both are too gray, though I love the trees and the coast around both. Salt Lake is too close and I dislike Boise. Denver is iffy, so I am thinking maybe Colorado Springs...find something Air-Forcey and live like Robert Heinlein."

Robert could tell Reva was joking. "Well, I'll certainly move to Colorado Springs if you want. But, maybe we should both go back to DC?"

Both sat back and pondered that suggestion.

Robert was happy this morning. He was beginning to think that he was healing better then he'd thought. After the incident, his body had healed first, then his mind, and then Jonesey and Jenny helped him heal his spirit. Lately, he'd been feeling emotionally better...less guilt, more contentment, and lately full-time sparks around Reva. He and Reva really sparked—they had great chemistry. Often he felt like he could short circuit and burn out at anytime. He wasn't sure they could make it the full two weeks of the agreed trial period.

This was their fifth morning in a row waking up at the same time, finding the fireplace and breakfast pick-me-ups together. He'd been sleeping better and could now go back to sleep after the nightmares. Sam was part of that; he'd jump on the bed when a nightmare grabbed Robert, and would stay until Robert got back to sleep, but Reva was part of it too. She had insomnia sometimes. He believed it was her brain. She would get thinking too hard and wake herself up. Sometimes she'd watch old movies on his Netflix, sometimes, she'd read, and once she'd snuck into his room and slept in the old recliner by his closet. He'd caught her, and asked her about it. She'd said she felt too lonely to sleep and hearing another human breath comforted her. He'd gotten out of bed and picked her out of the recliner to sleep next to him. She snuggled in a comforter on top of his blankets, and they ended up that way most nights since.

Jonesey had told him that Stan had said when he was in the hospital for the last surgery that Reva would haunt his hospital room at night. She was the only one who'd stay with him through the night, and he figured she must have gotten used to sleeping in a chair watching him in bed. That story made him think of how his grandmother watched over him when he was sick. He'd had a dream that took him back to high school, when he'd broken his arm at age sixteen while tubing (riding inner-tubes from tires like sleds) down a local hill with friends. His tube had been going too fast, gone off the track and slid down the snowy hill right into a tree. He'd been bounced off, but landed badly on his left arm. It had been a spectacular break...compound fracture, both bones in the lower arm and required surgery. He'd been in the hospital overnight. His mother had been hysterical, and less than comforting. Dad had made her go home and that night his grandparents had stayed with him in the hospital. He'd woken up in pain to find his grandma holding his hand on his good arm while the nurse dosed his pain meds. In the dream he found himself in this same position, and then his grandmother turned into his ex-wife, and then Reva. He then turned into his older self, with his damaged leg in the DC hospital. When the nurse left, Reva lay down by him on the hospital bed, which was somehow big like his bed here, and he'd gone back to sleep happily cuddled up with Reva.

Robert shifted to ease his discomfort from laying in the same spot for too long. He'd hoped being around Reva for these two weeks could feel like being around a roommate, totally platonic. But, no longer. He could smell her and lately found himself with a hard-on nearly all the time. He couldn't understand how he'd spent nearly three years impotent with the torment his body was feeling full time now. He smiled, thinking about the bounty God usually gives when he answers some prayers.

Robert had prayed for healing of that part of his body—he'd asked God about his condition and for relief. God always answers prayers, and his answer had taken time, but Robert had felt God tell him "It will come." Now, it looked like it had.

With Reva here Robert felt like he'd come back to life. Wherever he'd been, he was back...Getting up in the morning felt good. He looked forward to a new day, and lately instead of just getting to know her, he'd begun plotting of how he would *get* Reva. He'd liked her from the first. He loved her now and had totally enjoyed the first time she'd laid him flat when sparring. Now, she was quickly becoming his life.

He looked over at her. He could tell she was sleepy this morning. She'd said that on Sundays she would often get up early, but go back to bed and laze all day. This weekend they'd started having two Sabbaths each weekend. Reva's on Friday-Saturday, and Robert's on Sunday.

Today looked like a lazy kind of Sunday. She was wearing a bra, but had put on her pajamas instead of getting dressed. He'd bet money she'd be back in bed to lounge the minute they finished lunch. Robert thought of the women he knew. His sisters lounged when they were pregnant. His wife had never lounged, and his mother only lounged when she was sick. He considered Reva's schedule. She regularly slept for six to seven hours each night and was an active person every day, but Saturday. She'd used to spend Sunday as her recreation. He didn't know how recent her switching her Saturdays and Sundays change was, but Reva had said once, that she took Sunday as her day of rest like Jenny did, because she did her church on Saturday.

Robert knew that Jenny and consequently her household took Sunday's off. Jenny's herd went to church and ate their meals together, but it was quiet activities all day. Napping was allowed. Reading was encouraged and TV was limited to 'wholesome' stuff suitable for families. He'd seen Mitch turn the TV to home improvement shows and Disney movies.

He loved the soft Henley t-shirt Reva was wearing today. It was pink thermal, waffly material that made her skin glow, matched her cheeks, and darkened her hair. She had her hair in a long braid starting from her nape. He could see her ears and the line of her neck. She sat on the rug Indian style next to him. He looked at the line of her thigh. Robert knew that one day soon he was going to make a move and speed up their timetable.

He could tell that Reva felt the sparks too. Her pupils would dilate and her breath would catch. He also knew he could check her nipples, but hated doing that as it heated him up too far. He never actually made out with a girl in front of a fire and wondered if he ought to. He thought about all the TV and movie scenes he'd seen with a couple on a bearskin rug in front of a fire and wondered if it was as good as people portrayed it. He considered the soft braided rug they shared and the wood floors around. Reva yawned and stretched. She moved her empty mug over, stretched out her legs, and reached with her arms to her toes. He knew she'd be soon up for a snack or get up to go back to bed. Robert decided to make his move. He was tired of this halfway life. He wanted it all and Reva. He needed no more time. She was the one for him. He wanted to kiss her and see if he could make kissing Reva in front of the fire a daily/lifetime habit.

Reva wiggled her neck and stared at the fire without looking at him, "I think I'll go back to bed." She glanced over at Robert and saw he was staring at her. She looked flustered. "What?" she asked.

Robert's eyes sparkled. Reva was blushing. He answered, "You." He could tell Reva didn't know what he meant. So he decided to show her. Without looking, he set his mug behind him and turned to her. Her legs were stretched out in front and she was leaning back on her arms—slightly inclined back stretching her back muscles. At once Robert came over her. His leaned into her, his arms came around her, his hands resting on her hands. His face was close. Looking into her eyes, he said, "Miss Reva, I am looking at you. I've decided I want to marry you tomorrow or later today, and right now, I want to kiss you here and now in front of this fire."

As Reva was taking in what Robert said, he didn't give her time to answer. Instead his lips came down on hers. Soft and wonderful at first and then their mouths opened and lit on fire. They lay down flat. Hands went under shirt hems to touch smooth and hard and smooth and soft skin. Robert laid Reva down on the rug and let his hands roam free. Reva gave herself up to the kiss and used her hands, arms, legs and toes to open up to Robert.

When their need from oxygen overrode the hormones, Robert broke the kiss and took his bearings. Both hands where around Reva's head with most of his fingers in her hair having been working to pull it free from the braid. Both of their shirts had been pushed up so his bare stomach was against her bare stomach. He was laying half on his side and half on his back with Reva laying half across him. He could feel her soft breasts against his chest and her one leg was bent over his hip with their centers touching. He hadn't felt, but he would bet she was wet and ready for him. He could tell he was hard and pushing at her. Her lips were rosy and obviously kissed. He had to kiss her again, but he needed to get control of his body so he forced himself to slow down.

Softly he caressed her ears and her neck and he kissed her some more.

Reva broke the kiss this time. Panting and out of breath all she said was "Wow."

"Yeah, wow." he responded. "So, will you marry me now? I find myself in love with a beautiful woman, and with this beautiful woman on top of me, I find that I may disgrace myself." Robert continued, "I think you know where this is going, and I don't think we can wait the rest of the two weeks. When we finish this, we finish it right."

***

Reva smiled and lowered her head to rest next to Robert's cheek and neck to catch her breath. Many thoughts came her, but she voiced the loudest, "I would love to marry you today or tomorrow, sir. Preferably today, I don't want to wait any more, either."

Robert tightened his arms around her, "I know I can't walk, but I need to roll away so I won't ravish you where you lie."

"Hold on," she said to warn him.

Reva wiggled and contorted until she had an arm to brace herself, then she lifted her leg off Robert's hip and rolled onto her back. "I'll let you know when I am capable of moving." She said. "Let me know when it's safe to look to my left."

***

Robert laughed. He loved this woman. She was very pink, obviously turned on, and deeply embarrassed to look at what she later called his 'Tee pee' standing straight up. They both started laughing uncontrollably.

A few hours later found Robert and Reva at his church meetinghouse with his LDS bishop who agreed to marry them. The next day, they went to the county courthouse, got a marriage license, and were married at Robert's grandmother's house, with his father and grandmother as witnesses.

"I think it sparkles, like your eyes. It was my great-grandmother's." Robert said as he slipped the beautiful amethyst and gold ring on Reva's fingers.

In return she slipped a gold and copper twisted metal ring onto Robert's finger. "I hope we are always like your ring—permanently twisted together and welded tight!"

On the way home from Grandma's, they stopped by the post office and Reva dropped the forty-six wedding announcement cards in the blue box. Their friends and remaining family would find out about their marriage in the mail. It was good to be settled.

Reva spoke, "By the way, the moment it's warm this spring you need to take me down to the river so we can tell for sure that the dream we had was really a true dream!"

Chapter Thirty-Six
Just Another Day

In April two important letters arrived at Grandma's for Robert. One was a letter from Fran. She'd reconciled with Norman and would be marrying him in June and moving to California after all. She asked whether Robert was interested in a mostly restored Victorian house in Ogden. The second was from Stan with a newspaper clipping about the last Renata sentencing hearing. The nephew who'd shot Reva got fifteen years to life in Federal prison, while the lieutenant who'd admitted to the lavender IV plead out and got ten to twenty-five years for attempted murder of an FBI agent.

Later that night, Jonesey left messages on both Robert's and Reva's cell phones. They didn't get them until the next morning, because they had spent the day in bed like newlyweds will. By then it was too late.

***

Robert nudged the cabin door shut with his leg after shooing Sam back in the house. He and Reva were going to Denver today to arrange for shipment of her DC storage to Fran's Victorian in Utah. They had decided to live here in the summers, in Ogden the rest of the time, and work for Jonesey or Stan periodically, when FBI assignments called for it. Reva confessed that she'd loved Fran's house and she'd hoped he'd forgive her for being jealous of Fran. Robert had smiled and sent a message to Fran asking whether he could pay fair market value.

Fran's answer had been, "You made me happy when I was at my lowest. You also enabled me to meet Norman halfway, which has made me happier than I ever thought. You get the house as repayment for my happiness. Besides, I need the write-off for the loss."

Robert had closed his email and was checking his voicemail as Reva headed out to warm up the truck. It was still cold here in April, and it could still snow any day.

Robert was finally listening to Jonesey's voicemail on his way to the truck and heard his voice saying "The Renatas…" when the blast hit.

"Reva! Oh my God…Reva." Robert screamed in only the way a man could scream. Heat and flames blasted him in the face as he ran towards Reva's body sprawled on the driveway. The blast from the car bomb in her truck had thrown her back and to the side of the gravel drive, where she'd rolled at least twice before landing in a twist with her legs crossed at the knee and her left arm crumpled below her torso. Her right hand lay closest to him, and Robert noticed the fingers were scraped up, but none looked broken.

Gently he crouched near her checking the angle of her spine and neck trying to determine if her neck or back were broken. His fingers found her carotid artery and found the pulse.

"Thank you, Heavenly Father." Robert prayed out loud as he counted her heartbeats. Reva's pulse was fast and a little ragged, but steadily kept going.

Robert pulled back as he kept examining at her. Her right arm and both legs were at normal angles. It didn't look like any of those bones were broken. Her back and neck were also in natural, if strained positions.

Better call the ambulance in case of internal bleeding—and that break looks bad. He thought. Robert was pretty sure Reva's arm underneath was broken, and there was a good chance of head and internal injuries. He called 9-1-1, put his cell-phone on speaker in his pocket, and reached for her with both hands, holding her neck as steady as possible with his left hand and arm while using his right arm and body to turn Reva onto her back so he could check her arm and torso. He gave a quick report to the 911 dispatcher as he laid her back down and rushed into the house to grab something to splint the arm. He could tell

Reva had broken both the lower bones. Sam barked at him excitedly and he tried to pet him quickly. *Better let him out. He might be able to spot a clue besides.*

A few minutes later, Robert successfully splinted Reva's arm, but she was still out. *Probably a good thing. That arm will hurt like a mother.* Absently he stroked Sam's head as he sat on the gravel drive waiting for the EMTs to load Reva into the ambulance. The log on his phone showed Robert that the ambulance and EMTs had arrived in 12 minutes. *Not too shabby for a bunch of volunteers from Parachute.* They'd stabilized Reva as much as possible. They left the splint on her arm for the orthopedic surgeon to set at the hospital. He watched them load Reva and take off, lights flashing. Absently he thought, *They won't need the siren until they reach the main road.*

Thankfully the trauma team at Grand Junction Community hospital was first rate and used to traumatic injuries thanks to the nearby freeway and recreation areas. Reva was only lightly hurt, when compared to the other bombing victims he'd seen.

Sheriff Randal (Randy) Peters was on his way. He was a trusted family friend. He'd called to say he'd meet Robert within ten minutes to get his statement. Robert was torn between riding with Reva in the ambulance and waiting for Randy. Robert knew Reva would forgive him for not going with her. This was a crime scene and he needed to stay to help ensure no evidence was lost.

He also needed to stay so he could report his findings to his FBI buddies. He didn't want to think of the Denver FBI guys or Jonesey. Somebody would be here soon, he was sure. He'd called Jonesey, because of his message, but also because his was the only FBI contact in his new phone. By now Jonesey would have called the troops and would be on his way down. Mitch would probably have to make an appearance too.

"Good thing that I know the Denver guys. I think they'll also get somebody down here, Randy will know."

Reva's truck was still recognizable. Even with pieces missing and most of it burnt to black, it still held a relatively recognizable shape as a truck. The bomb had clearly been attached to the undercarriage at the rear of the engine compartment near the cab. The blast had blown through the firewall into the cab—up and out. The hood had blown up and then off in the force of the blast. The front tires were shredded from the back forward and mostly gone. He could see the axle and frame were still mostly there. The bending of the front fender was surreal. It looked like it had peeled forward from where it joined the doors. The glass allowed the shockwave to escape, but the doors and cab looked 'off.' Because the bomb was placed closer to the front doors' hinges, the doors stayed closed, but bulged out at the front where the strength of the hinges kept them in place. Only the heaviness of the truck frame and components kept so much of the structure.

Robert figured like many other car bombs, the truck bomb was set when the ignition turned. He felt Reva was still alive, because she'd started the truck with her remote fob, not by turning the key in the ignition.

Horror filled Robert as he pictured what would have happened had Reva been sitting in the driver seat when she started the engine.

The floor of the truck cab had blown up into the cab roof denting it up and out. The force pulled the cube of the truck cab into a pyramid shape. The tailgate was blown open, but was still attached. There was also a crater under the truck. The blast had lifted it up and then gravity had brought it down, flattening the rear tires. The rear of the truck bed and the outside of the gate still showed mostly the metallic blue of the paint—untouched by the fire. Irrelevantly Robert wondered whether the company that installed Reva's sprayed-on bed liner would be interested to see how well it survived the explosion.

Maybe they could adapt the coating for military vehicles to protect them from IEDs.

He'd have to check with his military buddies to share the findings. The liner helped the metal keep its shape and resisted the flames longer than the paint did. He was pretty sure GM would want to see the truck. He didn't imagine many 2013 GMC Sierras had been hit by car bombs, but he was sure that many government and law enforcement Chevy Surburbans and Cadillac Escalades had. He'd let Stan handle that.

Sam stayed close to Robert keeping him company as he reported to Randy, "She was walking out to the truck from the back of the cabin. I am pretty sure she hit the remote start so it could start warming up and the heater would kick on to warm up the truck. We'd been talking and I was following her out after shutting Sam inside. I came up to the kitchen and was coming to the front door when I saw her hold her keys out. The lights flicked on like they do when you lock the doors. It's a GM thing... Lock the doors and then hold down the remote start for a few seconds. Reva was still playing with this function and liked to hold the remote in her fingers and point her hand at the truck. A heartbeat, maybe two, and as soon as the engine turned over, BOOM."

The sheriff asked, "So, you think they weren't up on modern vehicles, and wired the bomb to the ignition?"

Robert responded, "I don't know. I have no idea why it went off with the remote start and not when she got in the truck. I know the remote start runs the engine for a time, even when you unlock the doors, but everything's locked until you put the keys in to the ignition and turn it to 'on.'"

"You know me, Randy. I'm old-school—no fancy stuff for me. The only remote start I had was an after-market job on my old Buick. It never worked and it shorted out my electrical system when I tried to disconnect it."

Randy asked, "But, you're sure it was a mob connection tied to your FBI stuff, or in response to your testimony?"

"It has to be. Neither Reva nor I have any other recent FBI confrontations that would do this. I'm sure there are folks who'd get her or me with a sniper, but car bombs aren't like any of our usual crowds. I just have a gut feeling it's the Renata guys…They must have saw our wedding announcement a few weeks back and then scoped us out to identify her truck. My FBI guys will check our angles and confirm or get back to you, though."

"Thanks, Robert. I'll wait here for my forensics staff and your FBI guys. Go to your girl."

"Thank you, Randy. Keep me posted."

***

Robert dropped Sam off at his mom and dad's and burned down the highway to the hospital. Twenty minutes later, he was in the emergency room. He spotted one of the EMTs at the desk and asked him for Reva's status.

"Robert, she stayed out the whole way here. They have her in the back with the doc. doing X-rays and scans to see what's broken—you did good with your splint. She should be okay." He patted Robert on the shoulder on his way out to the ambulance. Robert looked at the nurse sitting there, who looked up.

"Yes, we're still assessing things. Here's her purse and loose jewelry. Please fill out this paperwork, while I go check on her."

Robert guessed living in a small-ish town where everyone knew you was a good thing. He knew the nurse from high school, she'd had a class or two with his older brother. By now the staff knew he and Reva 'were FBI' and would cut some red tape for them hoping for a scoop on what happened. He figured they had about two hours before the first FBI suits got here to scare everyone quiet.

He knew he couldn't, but Robert wished they'd let him get into scrubs and go back with Reva immediately. Now that Randy had the scene under control with his forensics team starting the official investigation, Robert began to worry whether he should have come here with Reva. "What could I have done, but held her hand. Dammit, I wish I could have been with her to hold her hand." Recriminations and doubts about whether he should have stayed at the cabin or rode with Reva in the ambulance went back and forth through his brain.

Filling out the hospital paperwork helped kill time while waiting for the doctor's report. Robert rooted around in Reva's purse to find her insurance cards. He found her doctor's contact information in her phone. Automatically, he put down the cabin for her home address and frowned over the routine questions. Should he put down the date of her last period? Everyone knew they were newly married, but he wasn't sure if the husband should put that down. Robert pulled the amethyst ring he'd put on Reva's third finger and slid it on his pinkie. "She'll want it back as soon as possible, so I better keep it handy." *Wait. When was her last period?*

All of a sudden, Robert's brows wrinkled as he counted back. Reva came down from Ogden in late January or early February. He'd dragged her to his cabin about two days later. They'd lived together for about a week before marrying, and in all that this time, he'd never seen her use feminine hygiene products. Robert had a man's knowledge of periods from his twenty-plus years' experience as a normal, hormonally charged male, and had spent fifteen of them married to a woman who redefined 'bitch' once a month like clockwork. Reva had been staying with him in the same bedroom for the past two and half months. "We've been married for nine weeks. OMG. Double damn. She's either on something or her last period was ten weeks ago."

Robert knew he didn't have sufficient data to be sure, but realized this was a hell of a thing to think about at a time like this. Shit, he was forty-four and Reva was now forty-one having had her birthday in February. *There's only a small chance at our age anyway. Reva hasn't ever brought it up, and I didn't think to ask. It's even possible she did something before she got here—there's no way she'd start a new relationship without some sort of protection is there?* They'd never even used condoms… both being clean and having committed to each other.

Another nurse distracted Robert from his thoughts. "Robert, she's awake and asking for you. We have some time before the orthopedic surgeon gets here… if you want to follow me?"

***

Reva came to with the realization that she had a hell of headache and hurt all over. She lifted her arms to touch her forehead and felt the right one make it to her head as her world turned to pain from her left elbow down. Her eyes popped open, and she realized that her left eye was swollen, nearly shut. She began assessing the situation. Her body ached and hurt in various spots, but knees and toes were wiggling. *Fingers on right hand okay. Right shoulder okay. Left shoulder okay, so long as it doesn't move the elbow or lower. Stiffness from the old gunshot, but rest of shoulder is okay. Quick look, yes, the arm is there and five fingers, but that's one hell of a homemade splint.*

Reva recognized her 1-inch thick GMC Truck Parts Catalog and strips of duct tape. It seemed that Robert had grabbed duct tape and the catalog to splint her left arm. She was sure, now, that it was broken and badly. *Screaming pain like that, plus a feeling of grinding in the bones. It's definitely broken.* She knew that feeling. Last time she'd broke this arm, she'd felt like this. It was after the explosion in London…ten plus years ago. She'd bet she'd broken the arm in near the same places just above or below the new bone. Damn. Then she looked at her relatively fine left hand and noticed her ring was gone.

"Double damn, where is my ring? ... Dummy, they take of your jewelry in the hospital."

Reva reconsidered her priorities. Other than her arm and some aches here and there, she felt ok. "Don't worry about the damn ring. Where's Robert, I wonder. Better move on to other checks." Reva thought she thought that, but was talking out loud as she continued her health catalog. She felt the oxygen tubes in her nose. She felt the tape and IV in her arm. She was on a gurney, slightly elevated at the top, but must be in the emergency room. It was noisy and there were curtains around her. She felt dirty and gritty. What skin showed was scraped, bloody, and dirty with sand and grit. She was pretty sure that her entire back and left leg were covered in road rash. It felt hard to breathe, like she'd had the breath knocked out of her. She tried to remember, *What happened?*

She closed her eyes and concentrated, "I remember leaving the basement after drying some clothes and heading out to start the truck, while Robert checked his email and 'kenneled' Sam."

Reva could remember holding her remote button down to start the truck and then the next thing was the sensation of flying through space and then nothing. Hoping that she wasn't sedated meant that that they were still evaluating her and not that she was bleeding internally or had a concussion, Reva tried to turn her head to see if anyone was around. From her left outside the curtain, she heard.

"Doc, I think she's coming to, I'm going to get the husband."

The doctor pulled the curtain out of the way with an irritating scratching sound, "Miss Reva. You are one lucky lady. How are you feeling?"

***

Robert came up to Reva's gurney as she was explaining to the doctor, "No, I am probably NOT pregnant. I'm not at all regular, but my OBGYN says it's because my pipes are slowing down. Where's Robert and when the hell are you guys gonna get me some meds?"

The end of her statement was nearly a shout, but in Robert's expert opinion held part of sob. He'd worry about the P word later. For now, here was Reva awake and well enough to shout, which meant she's going to be all right. He rushed to her side and grabbed her right hand as he kissed her forehead. "Sweetie, it's good to see you alive."

Reva started to speak, but couldn't. Instead, tears ran down her cheeks as she cried.

Robert pulled a chair over and kept a hold of Reva's good hand as silent tears escaped her eyes as she stared at him. The orthopedic surgeon was on his way, ETA about an hour. The ER doctor knew that there wasn't much they could do for now, and closed the curtain to give them some privacy. Robert and Reva sat silently letting the feelings of the day wash over them.

That's how Jonesey and the Denver boys found them a few minutes later. Robert heard Jonesey as if he was in another room,

"If only we'd caught the last Renata nephew last night instead of this morning. Little bastard escaped the inmate bus and killed two prison guards doing the transfer."

Epilogue

"I'm not sure I can do this." Reva balked at the front door.

"Relax, honey. I'll handle your grandma, you stay with your mom and dad."

Robert hoisted the baby carrier to his right hand, and grabbed Reva's hand with his left. Together they climbed the steps to the building lobby and buzzed Rex's, Reva's dad's apartment. They had three days left of their ten days in Tel Aviv, and Reva's grandmother had finally agreed to see them. Reva figured she only wanted to see Joshua.

Tina, Reva's mom, answered the buzzer. "Hey kids, come on up."

Rex met them at the door. "It's so great to see you."

Hugs were exchanged. The baby was passed from his dad, to his Uncle Artie, Aunt Mari, and then his grandma. Tina loved him. And the whole family was overjoyed to see Reva so settled and with a baby of her own.

Rex met Robert's eye, "She's waiting for you in the den."

"I'm on it." Robert guided Reva over to her mother and they went into the living room of the flat to play with the nieces and nephews.

Rex handed Robert Joshua, and Robert went to face the dragon. "Hello, Grandma Rose, would you like to meet Joshua?" Robert entered the den to see his wife's grandmother standing next to the window looking outside.

Rose turned and for the first time looked on the man her granddaughter had married. Robert couldn't tell what she was thinking. The worry line between her eyebrows could be old or new. Her dark eyes gave nothing away.

She sighed and met Robert halfway. "Let me see

him."

Rose held Joshua up so they could look eye-to-eye. He was a beautiful baby. He had the same brown eyes and brows of his papa, but that chin, that mouth, and those ears belonged to Rex. "He looks a lot like Rex did at this age. He clearly got that chin from Reva." She remarked.

Holding the baby seemed to calm her. Rose nodded to Robert, sat down on one end of the couch, and settled the baby on her lap. "Let's talk, young man."

Robert sat down next to her. They began talking about life and the choices he and Reva were considering as both took turns paying attention to Joshua.

Robert tried to explain their plans about religion, "We're still looking into options. For now, we're going both to my church and to temple. Both Reva and I want to get closer to God, we just haven't decided which way is better, your way, or my grandmother's way." Robert opened the conversation.

Rose was content to let him talk. All the fights she'd had with Reva over the years hadn't brought Reva back into the faith, maybe this man could.

"Joshua really cemented it for us. He's such a blessing. I never expected to have kids, and God gave me both Reva and my son, I owe him for that and so much more. And face it, for now, you know that Joshua belongs to your way as his Mom's Jewish." Rose and Robert shared their first genuine smiles.

It was a good start.

About the Author:

Virginia lives in Northern Utah where she works full time when she's not writing books. Her husband and her cat keep her constantly entertained the rest of the time.

Acknowledgements:

Thanks to Mamma Marene, my buddies at work, and my Bab for helping me get another one done. I'm not a one-trick-pony thanks to you!

Social Media Links:

Facebook:
www.facebook.com/RevasRiver

Email: VirginiaBabcockBooks@gmail.com

www.ingramcontent.com/pod-product-compliance
Lightning Source LLC
Chambersburg PA
CBHW051137020726
47501CB00005B/1545